Camp Club Girls

Bailey and the
SANTA FE SECRET

© 2011 by Barbour Publishing, Inc.

Edited by Jeanette Littleton.

ISBN 978-1-60260-404-9

Cover design: Thinkpen Design

Published by Barbour Publishing, Inc., P.O. Box 719, Uhrichsville, Ohio 44683, www.barbourbooks.com

Our mission is to publish and distribute inspirational products offering exceptional value and biblical encouragement to the masses.

 Member of the
Evangelical Christian
Publishers Association

Printed in the United States of America.

Dickinson Press Inc., Grand Rapids, MI 49512; February 2011; D10002688

Camp Club Girls

Bailey and the
SANTA FE SECRET

Linda McQuinn Carlblom

BARBOUR
PUBLISHING

Strangers in a New Land

"What was that?"

Nine-year-old Bailey Chang jumped at the snort she heard behind her and twirled around.

Elizabeth Anderson, her fourteen-year-old friend from Amarillo, Texas, grabbed her hand. Sweat beaded on her pale forehead. "I don't know."

They inched toward a clump of dried bushes in the New Mexico desert. The pungent odor of livestock grew stronger as they approached the bushes. The hot August sun beat down on their sleeveless arms and necks, and a trickle of sweat rolled down Bailey's back.

"Smells like my grandma's farm!" Elizabeth held her nose.

Bailey covered her nose and mouth with her hand. "Maybe even *worse* than a farm." She saw the brown bush move. "Something's in there." Her slight frame trembled like a bowl of jelly.

Suddenly, with a squeal and a grunt, a bristly gray javelina charged stiff-legged at them from behind the bush and ran across the landscape. The girls screamed and bolted in the opposite direction, just as terrified as the wild pig. They didn't stop running until they got to Halona Tse's home, nearly a half-mile away. Halona was a distant cousin to Bailey and her mom.

"Whoa, what's the matter?" Halona said as they burst through the door.

Bailey, her mom, and Elizabeth had come to help Halona with her pottery shop just that morning, and the girls had gone out exploring the barren territory around her house. It was so different from Peoria, Illinois, where Bailey lived, or Amarillo, Texas, where Elizabeth lived.

"We came face to face with a fanged pig!" Wheezing, Bailey pulled her inhaler from her jeans pocket and breathed in the medicine to open her airway.

Halona laughed. "Sounds like you saw a javelina."

"He was so ugly." Elizabeth shuddered. "Gray and black bristly hair, little stiff legs, and an underbite like he needed braces!"

Bailey let out the breath she'd been holding since using her inhaler. "Yeah, he was a real beauty." She giggled. "But boy, could he move fast!"

"I'm just glad he didn't chase us, or I would have freaked out," Elizabeth said.

"You weren't freaked out?" Elan, Halona's thirteen-year-old son, smirked at Elizabeth. His build was small, but he had a handsome face and a winning smile. His long black hair was pulled back into a short ponytail that reached just beyond his shoulders. "You could have fooled me."

"Well, maybe just a little," Elizabeth admitted with a smile.

"We're used to seeing javelinas," Elan's younger sister, Aiyana, said. "We've grown up around them." Her black eyes sparkled, and her soft, black curls fell like a waterfall down her back. At eight years old, she stood nearly as tall as her brother.

"But you still have to be careful," reminded her mother. "Wild boars are not to be taken lightly any more than rattlesnakes are."

The color drained from Elizabeth's cheeks. "Rattlesnakes? I'm petrified of snakes."

"They're all over the place, but we don't see much of them." Elan acted like it was no big deal. Though he didn't stand much taller than Aiyana, he behaved as if he were ten feet tall. "But they're hiding out there. It's part of their defense mechanism."

Bailey's mom chimed in. "I'm sure you won't see one while we're here, Beth. I've never spotted one yet in all the times I've visited."

"Why don't you live closer to town?" Bailey asked, sitting next to Elizabeth on the couch. "Then you wouldn't have to worry about those things as much."

"We Native Americans have our own land to live on. It's

called a reservation. We even have our own government completely separate from the United States. We're a nation of people living among your nation, but our land is our own. We like to live out here where it's peaceful and quiet. Some of us work in town, though. My pottery shop is in Santa Fe."

"I can't wait to see it." Bailey looked around the Tses' small home. It was sparsely furnished and clean. Family pictures hung on the wall, but little else. The green plaid couch reminded Bailey of furniture she'd seen at secondhand stores, but she liked how soft it was and the way she sank down into it when she sat. Pottery lined a display shelf and sat on tables. "You have a lot of pottery here, too."

"We've made pottery for generations. It's one of our native crafts."

Elizabeth gazed at a brown pot with black swirls painted around it that sat on the coffee table. "This one is beautiful. Did you make it?"

"No, my mother made that one." Halona's eyes misted, and she smoothed her blue cotton dress. Her long black hair was pulled back into a bun at the back of her head. Streaks of gray made it sparkle like icicles on a Christmas tree. "She was a master at the pottery wheel. The best I've ever seen. I'm trying to keep the shop going now that she's gone, but it's so hard to keep up with everything during the heavy tourist season."

Halona's eyes got a faraway look. "My husband died when Aiyana was just a baby, and I didn't think I could go on. But my mother helped me keep the shop going. With her help, we somehow made it. Then when she passed away, I thought I could never do it alone. We've managed until now, the busy season. I can't thank you enough for coming to help us."

Bailey felt a stab in her heart. *It must be awful to lose your mother, even if you're already grown up*, she thought.

"How long has it been since your mother died?" she asked.

"Six months, though it seems only yesterday." Halona smiled weakly and looked at her children. "But I have good help. Elan is almost a man at thirteen. And my Aiyana does so much for me even though she is only eight. She lives up to the meaning of her name, 'ever blooming.' I never hear a word of complaint from her."

"It's a beautiful name," Elizabeth said.

"Names are very important in the Native American culture," Halona said. "We give great thought to what they mean. Elan's name means 'friendly,' and mine means 'of happy fortune.' I keep reminding myself of that when times are tough and I struggle to pay my bills."

"That's cool," Bailey said. "Mom, what does my name mean?"

Bailey's mom shook her head. "I'm sorry, but I don't know. We just liked the way it sounds."

Bailey sighed. "I'll have to look it up sometime, I guess."

"I know what my name means," Elizabeth said. "I was named after Elizabeth in the Bible, John the Baptist's mother. It means 'God-directed.' But sometimes people call me Beth, for short."

"Wow." Aiyana's eyes shone. "That's a beautiful name, too."

"Yes, it is," Bailey's mom said. "Halona, hopefully we can be of some help to you while we're here so it won't be so hard for you to live up to your name."

"So when can we see your shop?" Bailey asked.

Halona laughed. "Right now, if you'd like. We didn't open it up for the day yet since you were coming, but now that you're here, you can help us."

"All right! Let's go!" Bailey jumped up off the couch.

The group piled into Halona's big white Suburban and buckled up. It was an older vehicle, with windows you had to crank up and down. The dark blue backseat upholstery was torn on the passenger side. Aiyana rode in the front seat with Halona and Bailey's mom, and Bailey sat between Elan and Elizabeth in back.

Dust flew as they rode down the dirt road from the reservation to the paved main road. Bailey was awed by the rugged majesty of the Sangre de Cristo Mountains that ran alongside them. Prickly pear cacti dotted the desert as they zoomed toward Santa Fe. Soon they were on the freeway and arrived in Santa Fe minutes later.

"It's amazing how different it is here from on the reservation." Bailey stared at all the specialty shops around her. People roamed the streets popping into the small stores to look at handmade jewelry, pots, and art.

Halona parked in front of a store bearing a terra cotta sign with blue lettering that said EARTH WORKS on it. "Here we are!" she said.

"Earth Works," Bailey said. "I like it!"

"We take clay, which comes from the earth, and make it into pottery," Elan explained.

"But we use much more than clay in our pottery." Halona unlocked the shop door. "We use precious stones and minerals from the mines, and even ropes, which are made from plants. So much of what we use in our work comes from the earth."

The musky aroma of incense greeted the girls as they followed Halona into the store. Elan went to the counter and lit a short incense stick that looked as if it was left over from the day before.

"What kinds of mines do you have in New Mexico?" Elizabeth asked.

"Turquoise, copper, gold, silver—there are all kinds of mines here," Elan said.

"And we own one of the turquoise mines!" Aiyana's dark eyes gleamed. Her red T-shirt and brown corduroy pants could have been a boy's outfit, but looked decidedly feminine on the pretty little girl.

"Well, sort of," Halona corrected. "Legend says our family once owned the Suquosa Mine, which was one of the largest turquoise mines. It is no longer in operation. And the deed to the mine has been lost over the years. We have no proof we own it."

"What if you found the deed?" Bailey asked. "Could you reopen the mine and use the turquoise?"

Elan jumped in. "If we found it, we'd be rich!"

Halona put her hand on her son's shoulder. "We are rich in other ways now. But yes, Bailey, it would help us immensely in our work."

Bailey shot a look at Elizabeth, who smiled and nodded. The two walked around the shop admiring the beautiful pots while Halona took Bailey's mother to the office to show her the bookkeeping system she'd be helping with.

"I've never seen so many kinds of pots," Elizabeth said. "Some have handles, some are tall, and some are short. Others are painted with bright colors and some earth tones."

"And I've never seen pots with gems embedded in them before," Bailey added. "Those are my favorite."

"Do you make the jewelry, too?" Elizabeth asked Elan and Aiyana.

"Some of it," Elan replied. "We make all the pots ourselves, but we buy some of the jewelry and blankets from other Native Americans."

"It must take hours and hours to make these things!" Bailey scanned the shop, taking in the variety of items.

"It does," Aiyana said. "That's why we need your help during tourist season."

"Mom feels bad if Aiyana and I have to work too much." Elan shrugged. "But I don't mind. I tell her I am not a kid anymore. I'm the man of the family, and it is my duty."

"What happened to your dad?" Bailey asked gently. "Was he sick?"

"He had cancer and died when Aiyana was only five months old," Elan replied. "So I'm the man of the house."

Bailey nodded. Her heart broke for Elan and Aiyana as an image of her own dad filled her mind. She thought about the way he had tossed her in the air when she was a tiny girl and the way he teased her now that she was older. She couldn't imagine what it would be like to grow up without him.

Elan stepped outside to sweep the front sidewalk, and Elizabeth moved to another shelf full of painted pottery. Bailey followed her until she heard voices yelling outside.

"Look at the boy doing girl's work!"

"Sweep, little girl. Sweep!"

Bailey glanced out the front window and saw some teenaged boys on bikes taunting Elan. He didn't look up at them, but his face reddened as he swept the sidewalk with hard, deliberate strokes.

How can they be so mean? Just because he's smaller than they are doesn't mean they should get away with talking to him like that. Don't they know his dad died and he has to help his mom?

"Beth, come here!" Bailey motioned her to the window.

Elizabeth immediately saw why Bailey had called her over.

"You'll never be man enough to get married!" one boy jeered.

"Good thing your people don't perform the ceremonial rite of passage anymore, or you'd never be declared a man. You'd be a little kid forever!"

That did it. Elan dropped his broom and put his hands on his hips. "You want to come over here and say that?"

"Sure, I'll say it right in your face." One of the bigger boys hopped off his bike, letting it fall by the road. The other boys straddled their bikes, waiting to see what would happen.

"Should we go out there?" Bailey asked.

The big boy reached Elan, and the two stood facing one another, inches separating them, though Elan stood almost a foot shorter.

"What did you say to me, Paco?" Elan said through gritted teeth.

"I said you'll *never* be a man." Paco spat the words slowly and deliberately. Then he shoved Elan.

Bailey burst through the door with Elizabeth and Aiyana close behind. None of the girls spoke, but glared at Paco.

"These your girlfriends, Elan?" Paco teased.

"Bailey's my cousin, if it's any of your business."

"Looks like she's come to do your fighting for you."

"We have not!" Bailey said. "Just leave him alone and get out of here."

"Who's gonna make me?"

"I am!" Elan pushed Paco so hard he staggered backward.

"Elan!" Aiyana yelled.

"Why you—" Paco steadied himself and grabbed Elan's shirt collar, flinging him to the sidewalk.

"Stop it!" Elizabeth stepped forward and stood face-to-face with Paco. She was as tall as he was. Bailey and Aiyana moved to Elan's side and helped him up.

Paco laughed and turned to leave. "Have a nice day—sissy!" He grabbed his bike by the handlebar and hopped on.

"You showed him!" Willy, one of Paco's friends, said.

"Yeah, he's such a shrimp you could have eaten him!" said another.

The boys rode away laughing.

"Are you okay, Elan?" Bailey asked.

"I'm fine." He brushed dirt off his pants.

"Who are those guys?" Elizabeth asked.

"Guys from my tribe who think I'm too small to be of any good." Fury blazed in Elan's dark eyes.

"Guess they don't know the measure of a man is inside him," Elizabeth said. "God judges the heart, not what a person looks like on the outside."

"Try telling that to them," Elan said. "They've been pestering me for years."

"Does your mom know?" Bailey asked.

Elan shrugged. "She did a few years ago. But I haven't told her it's still going on."

"I think we should tell her," Aiyana said.

"No!" Elan shot back. "Mama isn't to know anything about this. She has enough on her mind."

Aiyana lowered her head, her black hair falling around her face like a curtain.

"I'm sorry, Aiyana," Elan said. "I didn't mean to yell at you. But I can handle this on my own. I'm practically a man. One day they'll be sorry they messed with me."

Elizabeth cleared her throat. "The Bible says, 'Do not seek revenge or bear a grudge against one of your people, but love your neighbor as yourself.' It's not easy, but it's the best way to solve a problem with other people."

"That may be the way you do things, but things are different in our Native American culture." Elan frowned.

"Different?" Bailey asked.

"Your Bible also says, 'An eye for an eye and a tooth for a tooth,' doesn't it?" Elan asked.

"Yes, but—" Elizabeth began.

"So that's how we solve things around here. We believe in peace for a time, but if that doesn't work, then it's time to take action." Elan spoke as if no one could ever change his mind.

Bailey nodded. "We'll pray for things to work out."

"Oh, they'll work out," Elan said. "I'll prove to them that I'm a man."

"You don't have to prove anything," Elizabeth said. "They're the ones with the problem."

"Yeah, well I'll show them." Elan turned and stomped back into the store, ending the conversation.

Bailey glanced at Elizabeth and Aiyana. "You don't think he'll do anything crazy, do you?"

"I doubt it," Elizabeth replied. "He's just mad."

"Those boys make him mad all the time," Aiyana added. "He's never done anything about it before."

Bailey inhaled deeply and blew out her breath through her mouth. She hoped Elizabeth and Aiyana were right.

The Mystery of the Mine

Inside Earth Works, Bailey wandered the aisles looking at the pottery, trying to forget what she'd just seen and heard. Her fury at the boys slowly subsided, though a dull ache remained inside her. Soon her eyes were drawn to a pot sitting on a shelf in a hallway toward the back of the store. She slipped toward it to take a closer look.

The pot was round and full at the bottom, but tapered up to a narrow neck and out again to form a wider lip. Standing only about eight inches tall, it was painted in intricate detail. A sunset desert landscape—complete with prickly pear cacti, mountains, and tiny quail—encircled the wide, round pot belly. The painted sunset blazed in brilliant orange, yellow, and pink just behind the rugged mountain. The pot took Bailey's breath away. She reached out and touched it. Then she picked it up.

"No!" Aiyana yelled.

Bailey jumped, almost dropping the pot. She quickly set it back on the shelf.

"You can't touch that." Aiyana flew to her side, taking Bailey's hand to pull her an arm's reach away from the pot.

"I—I'm sorry." Bailey felt the weight of disappointment descend on her like a heavy Native American blanket. How she wanted to hold that gorgeous pot and examine every inch of its painted picture. "I—I didn't know."

Elizabeth went to Bailey. "Is it some kind of special pot?"

"It is a pot that has been handed down from generation to generation in our family."

"It's beautiful!" Elizabeth exclaimed.

"We keep it back here so no one bothers it."

"I could still see it from the main store area," Bailey said. "You might want to hide it better so no customers try to buy it."

"We would never sell it even if someone offered us a fortune for it." Aiyana's black brown eyes became serious.

"Even if they offered you a million dollars?" Bailey teased.

Aiyana shook her head. "Not even a trillion."

"Wow. I guess some things are worth more than all the money in the world." Elizabeth smiled at Aiyana.

Aiyana looked down, studying her small, nervous hands.

"Aiyana? Are you all right?" Bailey asked.

The girl nodded, still not looking at Bailey and Beth.

"You sure?" Elizabeth asked. "Did we say something we shouldn't have?"

Suddenly Aiyana looked up at the girls, a determined

fire in her eyes. "If I tell you a secret, do you promise not to tell anyone?"

Bailey and Elizabeth leaned in to hear what Aiyana would say. "Of course we'll keep your secret," Bailey said. "What is it?"

Aiyana stepped closer and said softly, "My grandmother used to say that this old pot held the key to riches."

"Riches?" Elizabeth sounded surprised. "Do you know what she meant by that?"

"I'm not really sure." Aiyana scrunched up her face in apology. "Maybe she meant it would remind us of our rich family background." She paused and scratched her head like she'd never thought about this so much before. "But Mama said *her* grandma always told her that behind the sunset our treasure awaits."

"Was she talking about this pot?" Bailey asked.

Aiyana nodded.

"'Behind the sunset our treasure awaits,'" Elizabeth repeated. "I don't know what that means."

"Me neither," Aiyana said.

"That's totally mysterious. Sort of reminds me of the pot of gold at the end of a rainbow. Maybe they used to keep their money hidden in it." Bailey looked closely at the pot, being careful not to touch it. She saw more detail every time she studied it. "Is that turquoise going around the bottom rim?"

"Yes," Aiyana said. "Mama said they were really careful to cut the stones to the perfect diamond shape and size, and they polished them to make them shine. Then they set the turquoise in melted silver and let it harden. When it cooled, they pressed the silver and turquoise band into the clay while it was still soft—or at least that's what she's been told. Of course the pot was made before she was born."

"It's gorgeous," Elizabeth said. "Your family does awesome work."

"I'm just learning to embed stones in the pots I make, but I've been making pottery without stones for a few years now."

"Do you still cut and polish the stones yourself?"

"We don't, but there are people in our pueblo who do it for us."

"Is turquoise the most popular stone to use?" Bailey asked.

"It is around here." Aiyana nodded. "Around here Native Americans like my family are practically famous for their turquoise work because our ancestors lived near turquoise mines. But a long time ago, there was no rain for almost two years, and they had to move closer to the cities."

"Wow," Bailey said. "Two years with no rain is hard to imagine. We hardly go a week without rain in Illinois!"

"The drought was hard on my family back then. They were experts at using turquoise in their jewelry and pottery, but they had to move away from the mines. They just couldn't survive out there without water." Aiyana looked around to be sure no one else was listening. "Remember that mine I told you my family owned?"

Bailey and Elizabeth nodded.

"It had the most turquoise of any mine in the area. And they say the turquoise was more beautiful than the stones in all the other mines."

Bailey shook her head. "Too bad the deed got lost over the years."

"That's for sure." Aiyana said sadly. "We'd have the biggest and best turquoise mine around."

Elizabeth's face brightened. "Maybe we can help you find it while we're here."

"How could you do that?" Aiyana asked. "It's been lost for hundreds of years."

"I don't know how we'll do it, but I promise we'll try." Elizabeth patted the girl's hand.

"Elizabeth and I are great at solving mysteries," Bailey told her. "We're even in a mystery-solving club called Camp Club Girls."

"You are?" Aiyana's eyes widened. "Have you solved any mysteries yet?"

Bailey laughed. "We've solved lots of them! We were all in the same cabin at Camp Discovery, and we solved our first one at the camp. We found lost treasure. Since then we've solved more than a dozen mysteries together!"

"Then maybe you'll be able to solve this one, too!" Aiyana's smile was filled with hope. "It would help my family so much if we could prove we own the old mine. We could reopen it and not have to pay other people for their turquoise. We'd get stones from our own mine and use them for free!"

"That would sure save your mom a lot of money," Elizabeth agreed. "Plus, she could sell turquoise to other people to use in their crafts, too."

"Aiyana, would you mind if we told the other Camp Club Girls the secret about the pot so they could help us solve the mystery?"

Aiyana hesitated. "I guess that would be okay. We don't tell many people, because we are afraid someone may try to steal the ancient pot from us. But I know you wouldn't do that."

"That's for sure," Beth said. "And neither would our friends. Besides, they don't even live in New Mexico."

"Do you know where the mine was located?" Bailey asked.

Aiyana's face fell, and she shook her head. "That's the other problem. We don't even know for sure which land is supposed to be ours, much less where the mine is."

"Hmm." Elizabeth screwed her mouth up. "That is a problem."

"Well, we'll do our best to try to figure it out and find out if there's really a mine on it. Hopefully we'll find the deed to prove your family owns it, too." Bailey crossed her arms and nodded as if that settled the matter.

●—●—●

That afternoon, Bailey and Elizabeth went into their bedroom at Halona's house and used their cell phones to conference call the other Camp Club Girls. Bailey sat at the head of the bed and Elizabeth at the foot.

"Hey girls, everybody there?"

"We're here!" everyone shouted together.

"Guess what? Beth and I are in Santa Fe, New Mexico!" Bailey announced.

"Santa Fe! How'd that happen?" McKenzie asked. McKenzie Phillips was a fourteen-year-old from Montana who was good at seeing people's motives behind their behavior, and loved to ride horses.

"My mom's distant cousin, Halona, is a Native American who lives here," Bailey explained. "Her mother died and she needed help to keep their pottery store going during the busy tourist season."

Elizabeth jumped in. "Bailey asked if I could come and help, too. I'm only out of school for another week, but we decided it would be a fun ending to the summer. Plus, since I want to be a missionary someday, my folks thought it would be good training for me to see the Native American culture up close and personal."

"Do you want to be a missionary to the Native Americans?" McKenzie asked.

"I don't know yet," Elizabeth replied. "But learning any new culture is good training."

"Sounds interesting," said Alexis Howell, a twelve-year-old from Sacramento, California, who was also known as Alex. "Met any cute boys?"

Bailey rolled her eyes at Beth and smiled. "No, but we've met some not-so-cute ones."

Elizabeth laughed. "Some boys were really mean to Bailey's cousin, Elan."

"Why were they mean to him?" Sydney asked. Sydney was the athletic girl of the bunch, a twelve-year-old from Washington DC.

Bailey shook her head, the frustration of the encounter washing over her again. "Because he's small for his age and was sweeping the sidewalk in front of the pottery shop. They said he was doing girls' work. Can you believe that?"

"Sounds like they're living in a time warp," Kate said. Kate was the whiz kid of the group, even though she was only eleven. She specialized in gadgets galore at her home in Philadelphia. "Men do all kinds of different things these days, just like women do. How old is Elan?"

"He's thirteen, but is not too much taller than his eight-year-old sister."

"I think those boys must not feel very good about themselves, or they wouldn't bother someone else over something so ridiculous," McKenzie said. "My mom says people often mirror their own fears in what they say to other people."

"I never thought of that," Bailey said. "But whatever the reason, they were sure mean. Poor Elan tried to stand up to them, but the biggest boy, Paco, pushed him down."

"Do his parents know they're picking on Elan?" Sydney asked.

"His mom knew at one time, but doesn't know it's still going on. And his dad died when he was very young."

"His little sister, Aiyana, wanted to tell her mom, but Elan wouldn't let her." Elizabeth pushed back her blond, wavy hair.

"Anyway, that's not the real reason we called." Bailey sat up straight on the bed. "We have a mystery to solve."

"All right! What is it?" Alex asked.

Bailey and Elizabeth told the girls all about the pot that was handed down from generation to generation.

"It's so beautiful!" Elizabeth said. "You should see it!"

"Yeah, it has a desert landscape painted on it," Bailey told them. "It has cacti and even little quail walking in a line. And a bright sun setting behind a mountain fills the sky with all kinds of colors. It's so cool!"

"Why don't you e-mail us a picture?" Kate suggested.

"We will," Bailey said. "I hope we can get a good shot of it. We aren't supposed to touch it. I found that out the hard way."

"Well, don't break any rules or anything, but do the best you can." Kate suddenly giggled. "Biscuit, stop!" More giggling. "I think Biscuit says hi. He's licking the phone. It's disgusting!"

Even Biscuit was part of the sleuthing team! The girls had found him at Discovery Lake, and though Kate kept him most of the time, he still found ways to help the girls solve mysteries.

"Sounds like nothing has changed much with Biscuit!" Alex said. "So Bailey, what's the mystery about? Does it have something to do with the pot?"

"Halona's family used to own land that had a huge turquoise mine on it," Bailey explained. "The problem is that the deed has been lost for hundreds of years."

"Not only that," Elizabeth added, "but they don't even know where the land is or if there really is a mine on it. Our job is to try to determine the location of both and find the lost deed that proves it's theirs."

"Man, that's gonna be hard!" McKenzie wailed. "I'm not sure we can do that."

"Hold it!" Elizabeth said with a smile. "Don't forget that with God, anything is possible."

"True enough," Alex said. "What's your cousins' last

name? Maybe I could research public records on the Web."

"Their last name is Tse." Bailey spelled it for her.

"Oh! We almost forgot to tell you an important clue to the mystery!" Elizabeth banged her forehead with the heel of her hand. "Elan and Aiyana's grandmother used to tell them that the pot held the key to riches. And their great-grandmother always said that 'behind the sunset our treasure awaits.'"

"Weird!" Sydney said. "That sounds like some kind of code."

"Could be." Bailey tucked her feet under her legs in crisscross style.

Kate piped in. "I remember learning in history that some Native Americans were code talkers in World War Two."

"Oh, yeah!" McKenzie said. "I learned that, too!"

"Well, maybe this is some kind of code, too." Sydney cleared her throat. "I'll research that angle."

"Great!" Elizabeth said. "I think we've got a good start."

"How long will you be in Santa Fe?" Alex asked.

Bailey licked her lips. "Today is Saturday, and we leave on Thursday, so almost a week."

"That doesn't give us much time," Sydney said. "We'd better get busy."

"Okay," Elizabeth said. "Stay in touch with anything you come up with, even if you're not sure it really applies to the case."

"Right," Bailey agreed. "That's what the police always say about tiny bits of evidence. If you know anything or saw anything that could possibly have something to do with a case, call. We'll try to put the pieces together later."

"Okay," Kate said. "Have fun in Santa Fe!"

"We will!" Bailey hung up and high-fived Beth.

The mystery solving had begun.

Becoming a Man

Monday morning, the Tses, Bailey, her mom, and Elizabeth went to open up the shop at eight o'clock. Bailey removed the black velvet coverings off the jewelry cases, and Beth dusted the pottery. Aiyana swept the floor while Elan turned on soft Native American music. Bailey's mom retreated to the back office with a steaming cup of coffee to work on the bookkeeping records that were weeks behind.

"When you're done dusting, let's look at that pot again," Bailey suggested to Elizabeth.

"I don't know, Bales," Elizabeth replied. "Maybe we should just leave it alone."

"We won't pick it up," Bailey said. "But it can't hurt to look at it. We told the girls we'd get pictures of it to send them."

"Okay, but we have to be careful." Beth tickled a pot with her feather duster. She finished dusting the row of merchandise and returned the duster to the closet. "I'm done. Are you?"

"Yeah, I'm done, too." Bailey hopped off a high stool behind the counter, and the two walked to the back of the store.

"Let's get those pictures taken and then get away from here." Elizabeth pulled out her phone and held it close to the ancient pot. "I hope the lighting is good enough."

"Guess we'll find out," Bailey said.

Elizabeth clicked the picture and then showed Bailey. "What do you think?"

"It's a little dark, but I'm sure they can still see it," Bailey said. "It only shows part of the painted picture, though. I'll turn it one quarter of the way around so they can see the continuation of it."

"Bailey," Elizabeth said in a warning voice. "We shouldn't touch—"

But it was too late. Bailey had already reached out and turned the pot.

"See? I was careful," Bailey assured her friend.

Elizabeth snapped a shot of the pot in its new position, and Bailey gave it another one quarter turn. Soon they had four pictures that showed the entire desert landscape to send the other girls.

"I'm glad that's done." Elizabeth wiped imaginary sweat from her forehead.

"You worry too much," Bailey said. "How could I break it when I wasn't even picking it up?"

"I know, but I hate to take chances." Beth blew a strand of hair from her face. "Anyway, it's done, and nothing happened. I'm praising God for that!"

The two laughed.

"Hey, what's this?" Bailey looked into a room across from the office where her mother was entering data on a computer spreadsheet.

Halona and Aiyana came to the back of the store just as she asked.

"That's our studio," Halona said. "I teach pottery classes in there."

Bailey's dark almond eyes widened. "You do?"

Halona nodded. "Pottery making has been in my family for generations, so it comes naturally to me. We even follow pueblo tradition of making our own dyes from plants and other parts of nature."

"Wow. That's amazing," Bailey said. "Who do you teach it to?"

"Anyone who wants to learn." Halona smiled broadly.

"Could you teach me?" Bailey asked.

"I could *start* teaching you," Halona replied. "There's a lot to learn in the short time you'll be here."

"That's okay," Bailey answered. "I'll learn as much as I can, and then maybe I could take more lessons at home. Do you want to do it, too, Beth?"

"Sure!" Elizabeth shrugged. "Sounds like fun."

"When can we start?" Bailey asked.

Halona peeked down the short hallway and into the shop. "Well, it looks like we don't have any customers yet, so how about now?"

"All right!" Bailey raced into the studio and took a seat at the table.

"Before you get too comfortable, put on a smock," Halona said.

"Yeah!" Aiyana said. "Pottery making can get pretty messy."

"Elizabeth, do you have a tie so you can keep your hair out of the way while you work?" Halona asked.

Elizabeth pulled an elastic band from around her wrist. "I always keep these handy." She quickly smoothed her long, medium-blond waves into a ponytail.

"You'd hate to have to do that after you've started, or you'd have wet clay stuck in your hair." Aiyana laughed and finger-brushed her own dark curls back and secured them in a scrunchy. "Believe me, I know!"

"See?" Bailey tucked her chin-length, silky-black hair behind her ears. "We're learning things already!"

Elan appeared at the door and peered in. "What's up?"

"We're going to take pottery lessons from your mom." Bailey spoke as proudly as if she'd just gotten an Olympic gold medal.

"This I've got to see." Elan flipped a chair backward and straddled it, his tan arms resting on the back. His black hair hung loose today, and he flashed a grin at Elizabeth, causing her to blush. Bailey had to admit her cousin really did look good in his blue jeans and brown T-shirt. He chuckled. "Let the show begin."

"First, we need to lay out this canvas so your clay doesn't stick to the table." Halona whooshed the fabric out over the table like a clean sheet over a bed. "And now you each need a chunk of clay."

Halona retrieved a block of gray clay and removed the plastic wrapping that surrounded it. She sliced a hunk off for Bailey and one for Elizabeth, plopping them down in front of the girls with a dull thud.

"Now, roll and press the clay to change its shape from a rectangle into a ball," Halona instructed. "This will also help soften it and make it easier to work with."

Bailey pressed and rolled the clay. "This is so much stiffer than the modeling clay I used to play with when I was little."

"No kidding." Elizabeth stood to put her full weight on her glob of clay. "We're going to get strong doing this!"

"Yes, it takes strong arms and hands to be a potter." Halona watched the girls' progress, giving tips as they worked to soften the clay.

"This makes me think of where the Bible talks about God being the Potter and us being the clay." Elizabeth rolled her clay on the table. "I wonder if I'm ever as stubborn as this clay is."

"My mom says I have a strong will." Bailey worked her clay. "It can be bad, like if I'm stubborn and want to do things my way instead of God's way. Or it can be good, like when I'm strong enough to say no to a group of kids who want me to do something I shouldn't."

Elizabeth nodded, and Bailey continued. "Like once some of my friends thought it would be funny to place an order at a fast food drive-through window and then run the other way before the workers had time to see us. I told them it wasn't funny to play jokes like that and we could get into trouble. It's like stealing people's time, and you can't give that back. Then I just walked away."

"What'd they do?" Elizabeth turned her clay over.

"Most of them went ahead and did it anyway, but one other girl walked away with me. She seemed glad to have someone to help her stay out of trouble."

"You did the right thing. I guess the main thing is that we're soft and moldable so God can make us into who He wants us to be." Elizabeth flipped her ponytail back, and then shoved the heel of her hand deeper into the clay.

Bailey stood back and looked at her clump of clay with a smile.

"What?" Elizabeth asked.

"I was just thinking. What if my pot said, 'I don't want to be a bowl? I want to be a vase.' And it wouldn't let me make it into what it was meant to be?" Bailey laughed at her own idea. "I guess sometimes I say that to God."

Elizabeth laughed. "I'm sure we have lots of learning to do about being moldable clay for God to use and about making actual pots from clay. I want to be a useful vessel for God, not just a hunk of unmanageable clay!"

The girls kept working their clay until, finally, their rectangular pieces were smooth, round balls.

"Good," Halona said. "Now push your fingers into the middle of the ball to make a nice indentation. This will be the start of your bowl."

The bell on the front door dinged, announcing Earth Works' first customer of the day. "I must tend to the customers. Elan, you stay here and help the girls."

"No problem." Elan stood and laced his fingers, then stretched his arms out, cracking his knuckles. A smile played on his lips as he pulled a narrow strip of leather from his pants pocket and tied his hair back. "I'll teach 'em how it's done."

Aiyana rolled her eyes. "Puh-lease."

Under Elan's direction, Bailey and Elizabeth molded their clay balls into dishes, dipping their fingers in a small bowl of water to smooth the rough spots.

"That's neat that your family makes their own dyes," Bailey said. "And it's earth friendly, too."

"Native Americans have always been earth friendly,"

Elan replied. "The rest of the nation could learn a lot from our ways."

Beth smoothed the side of her pot. "Seems like you have a lot of cool traditions you still practice."

"Yes, we do," Elan said. "But we also have some that have fallen by the wayside."

"Like what?" Bailey asked.

"Well, for instance, we used to have a rite of passage for boys when they turned thirteen."

"Rite of passage?" Bailey gave him a look. "What's that?"

"It's when you're declared an official adult of the tribe." Elan thought for a moment. "It means you're not a little kid anymore, and you have adult responsibilities."

"I've heard of other cultures that do that, too," Elizabeth said.

"Do you have to get a job and not go to school anymore?" Bailey asked.

"No, not like that," Elan said. "The boys had to prove themselves."

"Prove what?" Bailey looked at Elan like he was slightly crazy.

"Prove that you're ready for manhood."

"How?" Bailey asked.

"The boys used to have to climb the rock face by the Puye Cliff dwellings by hand—no ropes or tools allowed."

"That sounds dangerous!" Beth said.

"That's part of the reason they don't do it anymore." Elan's face dropped a bit, and Bailey sensed his disappointment. "It's a sheer cliff, straight up and down, with only a few hand- and toeholds for men to pull themselves up with. The whole tribe would come to watch and cheer on the boys. Now they just have a special ceremony for us and perform a rite of passage dance to say you've become a man."

"Did anyone ever fall from the cliff?" Elizabeth's eyebrows lowered over her hazel green eyes.

"Sometimes," Elan said. "But then that gave them the chance to show their bravery through injury. It still proved their manhood. No one ever died."

"Did you already have your rite of passage ceremony?" Bailey dipped her fingers in the water and back to her clay.

"Yeah, they did it a few months ago."

"So you're officially a man now?" Beth asked, color rising to her cheeks.

"I guess," Elan said. "I don't feel any different."

"Well, I'd say you're a man whether you feel like it or not." Bailey looked up from her project. "You had your rite of passage, and you already have a job."

"Yeah." Elizabeth nodded, her color returning to normal. "You even help take care of your mom and sister. You definitely have adult responsibilities."

"I wish the boys at school could see it that way." Elan's

voice was soft and low.

"What difference does it make?" Bailey said. "What they think doesn't decide who you are."

Elan paused and seemed to think about what Bailey said. "I still wish I'd had the chance to prove myself on that cliff. That would settle it once and for all."

"Unless you fell and cracked your head open," Bailey said. "Then you'd be sorry you took the chance."

"I'd show them I could take it like a man." Elan sat up tall and puffed out his chest. "Maybe one day I still will."

"Now you're talking crazy." Aiyana was much further ahead in shaping her bowl than Bailey and Elizabeth were.

"What's so crazy about it?" Elan asked his sister. "Hundreds, maybe even thousands, of boys have scaled the Puye Cliff dwellings. People used to live in them!"

Aiyana eyed him smartly. "Yeah, but they're closed to the public now because it's too dangerous."

"They're closed to the public because people were damaging the old cliff dwellings," Elan corrected. "They want to preserve them for history."

"*And* because it's too dangerous," Aiyana countered. "Mama says people were afraid they'd get taken to court if someone climbed up there and fell."

"Sounds like there were several reasons to close the cliff dwellings to the public," Elizabeth put in. "I'm sure you're both right."

Bailey breathed a sigh of relief that Elizabeth was stepping into the brother and sister squabble. She knew her friend was a great peacemaker, a quality she hoped she'd learn someday. But for now, she usually found herself inwardly cringing on the sidelines when people argued.

"Maybe you can take us to see the Puye Cliff dwellings sometime," Elizabeth said. "I've never seen ancient rock houses before."

"Sure, we can go there. But they have most of it fenced off now, so we can't get as close as we used to." Elan checked Elizabeth's bowl. "This is looking pretty good. But you don't want to make that side too thick," he warned. "It will crack in the kiln if it's thicker than the rest, because it won't dry evenly."

Elizabeth smiled. "Okay, thanks."

"So what do we do next now that we have our bowls shaped?" Bailey asked.

Aiyana jumped in before Elan could answer. "We take them outside and set them in the sun until they're bone dry."

"Do we get to paint them?" Bailey asked.

"Eventually," Aiyana replied. "After they're dry we'll glaze them. That's what the paint's called."

"How long does it take them to dry outside?" Elizabeth asked.

"Usually a day or two." Aiyana looked at the bright sun beaming through the window. "When it's this warm outside, probably only a day."

The door dinged again, and Elan stood. "I'd better go help Mother with the customers."

"Thanks for helping us get this far." Bailey waved as he left.

After the boy had left the room, Elizabeth asked, "What do you think about what Elan said?"

"What do you mean?" Aiyana tilted her head.

"Do you really think he'd try scaling the Puye Cliff dwellings?" Elizabeth's eyes were clouded with concern.

"No." Aiyana sounded sure of her answer. "He's talked of doing that plenty of times before. He'd never do it. It's way too dangerous."

Bailey picked up her bowl and followed Aiyana toward the back door.

"Do you think we should say anything to your mom about it just in case?" Elizabeth scooped her dish up and went with them.

"No, I'm sure he's just talking big." Aiyana held the door for the girls. "We've got nothing to worry about."

Elizabeth didn't look so sure. "I hope you're right."

Desert Wanderings

Back at the Tses' house that afternoon, Bailey flopped onto the bed and opened her laptop. Elizabeth sprawled out next to her. They sent the photos of the ancient pot from Elizabeth's phone to the other Camp Club Girls. It wasn't long before Bailey's phone rang. "Hello?"

"Hi, Bailey. It's Kate."

"Hi, Kate. Did you get the pictures?"

"Yes! You were right. That *is* a gorgeous pot. I love all the colors in the sunset!"

"Me, too. Hang on a second. I'll put you on speakerphone so Beth can hear, too." Bailey pushed the speaker button.

"Hi, Kate! It's Elizabeth."

"Hi, Beth."

"Anyway, back to the subject," Bailey said. "The sunset's my favorite part, too."

"I'm going to print the pictures out so I can research them. Biscuit!"

Elizabeth giggled when she heard Biscuit panting over the line. "Hi, Biscuit!"

"He's going nuts!" Kate laughed. "Get down, boy. Anyway, I'm hoping I'll spot a clue somewhere in the picture that you didn't pick up on."

"That would be great," Bailey said. "Let us know if you find anything."

"Okay. Will do."

"Okay. Bye." Bailey flipped her phone closed.

A knock on the bedroom door made Bailey sit up. "Come in!"

"Hey!" Elan said. " 'S up?"

"Not much. We just got off the phone with one of our friends from camp," Elizabeth said. "What about you?"

"I wondered if you wanted to go see the Puye Cliff dwellings." Elan held a floppy, off-white canvas hat, and his eyes flashed with excitement.

"Sure!" Bailey was off the bed in a flash. "Is your mom driving us?"

"No. It's not far. We'll walk."

"Really?" Bailey looked doubtful. "They're that close?"

"Well, it's a good hike, but I've done it plenty of times." Elan sounded so sure. But still, a little worry sat at the edge of Bailey's mind.

"Let us get some water bottles first," Bailey said. "I don't know much about hiking, but I know you should always take plenty of water."

The girls grabbed water bottles from the fridge and handed one to Elan, who put on the wide-brimmed hat he'd been holding. They tucked their cell phones in their pockets and were ready to go.

"Here," Elan said, handing them each a fanny pack. "We usually wear these when we hike so we don't have to carry water bottles. I also put a little bag of trail mix in each one in case we get hungry."

"Thanks." Bailey strapped hers on and slipped her water bottle into the mesh side pouch.

Bailey's mom was reading the newspaper in the kitchen. "Mom, we're going to hike with Elan to the Puye Cliff dwellings," Bailey said. "He says they're not far."

"Okay, be home for supper."

"We will. We have our phones if you need us." Bailey patted the pocket holding her phone.

"Have fun!" Mrs. Chang called.

The screen door slammed behind them as they started out. Every time she went outside, Bailey marveled that her cousin's house was so far in the middle of nowhere. A few other homes spotted the barren landscape, but Bailey noticed there weren't any stores like she was so used to in Peoria, Illinois.

Elan led the way through the dry terrain. "We have to walk this direction awhile, then you'll see the cliff dwellings." A lizard sunning itself on a rock scurried to safety under a creosote bush.

"Is this a desert?" Bailey asked.

"Not really. But it's typical of the southwest with its dry, hard dirt and gravel and tall, dry grass. Lots of scrubby bushes and big rocks, too. We have some cacti like prickly pear, but not the tall saguaros with arms you see in some deserts. Southern New Mexico has part of the Chihuahuan Desert in it, but Santa Fe's in the northern part of the state."

"We won't run across any snakes, will we?" Elizabeth asked.

"Probably not." Elan kept walking. "But you never can tell."

Bailey saw Beth's wide hazel green eyes scanning the desert for any sign of movement.

"If a rattlesnake was around, we'd know before we got too close," Elan said. "That's what the rattler is for—to warn people and tell them to get away."

Bailey saw the worry in Elizabeth's eyes. "Don't worry, Beth. Elan grew up out here. He'll take good care of us."

Elizabeth nodded but kept scanning the area.

"Are we near the cliff dwellings yet?" Bailey asked.

"A little farther," Elan said. "Up around those big rocks, then a little bit past that."

Bailey stopped and sipped her water. The sun was beating down without mercy. Only scraggly bushes and tall desert plants grew here with an occasional desert willow tree, which didn't provide much shade.

"We should have put on sunscreen," Elizabeth said. "I'll be burnt to a crisp."

Elan said, "Here. Why don't you wear my hat? At least that will shade your face." He whipped off his hat and tossed it to Elizabeth.

Beth looked at the floppy hat and laughed. "This will be a new look for me." She shoved it on and struck a pose. "How do I look?"

Bailey laughed. "Like a cross between a fashion model and a desert rat."

"I think you look great!" Elan said. "At least you won't look like a lobster when we get back."

"Not my face anyway." Elizabeth held her arms out and inspected them as they walked. "My arms, maybe. We'll have to try to take cover under some of the trees or tall rock formations."

"What time is it?" Elan asked.

Bailey checked her cell phone. "Three thirty-five."

"At least we're not in the most damaging rays. They're usually the worst between ten and two o'clock."

"Good point," Elizabeth said. "But then again I've heard the hottest part of the day is usually around five or six o'clock, just before the sun goes down."

"Hopefully we can get back before that," Bailey said.

"Yeah, I feel like I'm being barbecued." Elizabeth wiped

sweat from her forehead.

Elan stopped and looked around.

"What's wrong?" Bailey scanned the area, looking for signs of trouble.

"Nothing." Elan looked the other way.

"E-laan," Bailey said, drawing out his name. "Tell me what's the matter."

"Nothing! I just thought the cliff dwellings were right over there, but they're not. We must have gotten turned around when we stopped to take a drink or when I gave Beth my hat."

"How could we have gotten turned around?" Elizabeth said. "We barely even stopped."

"I don't know, but something's not right." Elan walked ahead, and the girls followed. "I think we need to go this way."

"Are you telling me we're lost?" Elizabeth said.

"Not lost," Elan replied. "Just turned around. We need to go toward those rocks over there."

Bailey followed Elan's finger to the rocks and saw them in the distance. "Clear over there? I thought you said the cliff dwellings weren't far?"

"They aren't if you take the direct route!" Elan's voice rose. "But when you're traveling with two complaining girls, it's easy to get turned around." Then he mocked them. "I'm hot. I'm getting sunburned. I need a drink. Are we almost there?" Then back to his own voice. "No wonder it's taking so long!"

"It's not our fault if it's taking longer than usual," Bailey shot back. "We've kept up with you step for step."

Elan stomped toward the distant rocks. Elizabeth and Bailey hurried behind him, determined to keep up with his faster pace. Bailey wiped the sweat from her face with her T-shirt sleeve. Elan was now ten feet ahead of them.

"Elan, slow down!" Elizabeth called.

But he continued, angry, toward his destination.

"Bailey, we'll never be able to keep up this pace." Elizabeth's face was red with heat.

"Let's stop and rest." Bailey sat on a rock and opened her water bottle, gulping the lukewarm water that filled her mouth.

"He'll wait for us when he sees how far behind we are." Elizabeth took a drink and sat beside Bailey. She put both feet on the rock and rested her head on her knees.

Suddenly, the girls heard a rattle. They looked at each other and froze in fear. "A snake!" Bailey whispered.

Elizabeth nodded, her face paling.

"We have to step away from this rock so he knows we won't hurt him," Bailey said. She slowly stood and took a giant step. "Come on, Beth!"

Elizabeth opened her mouth, but nothing came out.

"You can do it, I know you can!"

"I can't move!" Elizabeth finally squeaked.

"Yes, you can." Bailey held her hand to her friend. "First you have to stand."

"I'm afraid to put my feet on the ground. The snake may strike me!"

Bailey spoke in a calm, soothing voice. "No, he won't. I was sitting next to you when I got up, and he didn't strike me. You can do this."

The snake's rattle continued.

"You know snakes are one of my worst fears, Bales."

Bailey saw tears run down Beth's cheeks. "I know, but you can do everything through Him who gives you strength! We learned that verse at camp, remember? Philippians 4:13. It applies to situations we think are too hard for us. You can do anything with God's help. Even this."

Elizabeth closed her eyes and pointed her face skyward as if praying silently. She wiped the tears from her face, then inched her feet down the rock until her toes touched the ground.

"Good girl!" Bailey cheered quietly. "If that snake wanted to hurt you, he would have already done it. Now stand and take a step toward me."

Beth steadied herself against the rock as she slowly stood. Then she practically ran to Bailey's waiting arms.

"You did it!" Bailey hugged her friend.

"More like God did it," Beth said. "I couldn't have done that without His help."

"You are living proof of the verse we learned."

"That's for sure."

Bailey grew silent, and then she heard the rattle again. She saw the snake's head poke out from behind the rock, its tongue flicking the air. "Let's get out of here!"

Both girls took off running in the direction Elan had gone. They saw he had turned around and was coming back in their direction. When they started running, he ran to meet them.

"What's the matter?" he yelled.

"A rattlesnake!" Bailey screamed.

As they got closer, they slowed to an exhausted trudge.

"Why did you leave us?" Elizabeth scolded when they were close enough to talk. "We were practically bitten by a rattlesnake!"

"Because you were blaming me for getting us lost!" Elan looked away. "I'm sorry. I should have stayed with you. Are you all right?"

"We are now," Bailey said. "But the snake was hiding under the rock where we stopped to rest. Way too close for comfort."

"I've never been so scared in all my life." Beth shuddered.

"I'm sorry." Elan tugged at his ponytail. "I really am. But I do have some good news."

"You do?" Bailey said.

"The Puye Cliff dwellings are right past these boulders. We're practically there!"

"Finally!" Elizabeth said. "I don't know how much farther I could have walked."

"Yeah, we've been walking an hour in this heat already." Bailey lifted her hair off her neck, wishing it were long enough to pull in a ponytail.

"Come on." Elan extended his hand to show them the way. "Follow me. Some trees up here can shade us so it won't be as hot. I promise it's not far."

The trio hiked another ten minutes and just past the boulders, they saw the cliff dwellings. Some of the ruins were on the ground, remains of an ancient civilization. Handmade stone walls stood only about three feet high, but the three could still see the shape of rooms and buildings that had once stood there.

"Wow!" Bailey said. "This is amazing!"

"The Puye Cliffs were home to around 1500 Pueblo Indians in the late 1100s to around 1580," Elan explained. "Then the drought forced them to move to the Rio Grande River valley."

"Oh, yeah. Aiyana told us about the drought," Bailey said. "Are you a Pueblo Indian?" she asked Elan.

"Yes and no. The Pueblo Indians split into eight different pueblos when they had to move. We're known as Santa Clara Pueblo Indians," Elan replied.

"Look up there." Elizabeth pointed to the side of the cliff.

"Cliff dwellings!" Bailey said. "How did they ever build

them on such a sheer hill?"

"I'm not sure," Elan said. "It's even more amazing when you realize they didn't have modern equipment to help them."

"It looks like it has two levels." Elizabeth pulled out her phone and took a picture.

"It does," Elan said. "The people used ladders to go from one level to the next."

"It's like an ancient apartment complex!" Bailey laughed.

Elan pointed to the solid rock wall to the right of the cliff dwellings. "During the rite of passage, the boys would climb this side of the cliff without ropes or tools of any kind." He eyed the rock with awe.

Elizabeth shook her head. "I can't imagine how anyone ever did that."

"It wouldn't be that hard," Elan said. "I bet I could do it. You can see the handholds when you get up close."

"You'd do it or die trying," Bailey said. "How could any parent let a kid do that?"

"That's the point," Elan said. "They're not children anymore. They're becoming adults in the rite of passage."

"Seems like a silly tradition to me," Elizabeth said. "No reason to have to grow up overnight, especially by doing something so dangerous."

"Our traditions mean a lot to our people." Elan sounded offended.

"I'm sure you have many traditions that are worth keeping, but I'm glad this one fell by the wayside." Bailey patted Elan on the back. "I'd hate to see my cousin up there!"

Bailey and Elizabeth took more pictures of the ancient dwellings.

"What's that?" Bailey pointed to a mountain area not far from the cliff dwellings.

"That's where some of the old turquoise mines used to be." Elan shaded his eyes with his hand. "They're not open anymore. They were closed when the drought hit, too."

"It's sad what a lack of rain can do." Elizabeth looked around again. "Very cool, Elan, but we'd better get back now."

Elan looked at his watch. "Yeah, we've been gone almost two hours. It will be time for supper when we get home."

"I'm already getting hungry from all this walking." Bailey pulled out her bag of trail mix to munch on.

"Hopefully it won't take as long to get home as it did to get here," Elan said. "We'll try to stay on track this time."

"They should build roads to the cliff dwellings," Elizabeth said.

"They have, but they're on the other side going toward Santa Fe. None of them lead back to the reservation." Elan laughed. "I guess they figured Santa Fe tourists wouldn't want to hike all the way out there."

"Probably a good guess. It was far enough coming from your house." Bailey pulled her cotton candy flavored lip balm out of her pocket and smeared some on her parched lips. "Anyone else need some?"

"I'll take some." Elizabeth applied the lip balm. "Mmm. This makes me think *food*!"

"Thanks for taking us to see the cliff dwellings, Elan," Bailey said. "They're really neat."

"Yeah, and I even got to meet a rattlesnake!" Elizabeth laughed. "Not that I want to ever do it again!"

"I'm glad you got to see them." Elan gulped down a drink. "I go there fairly often. It doesn't seem that far to me, but I guess it is for people who don't hike that much."

"If I were you, I wouldn't take that hike alone, Elan," Beth said.

"What if something happened?" Bailey added. "You'd be stuck out there with no one to help."

Elan waved the mother hens off with his hand. "I've hiked alone plenty of times. I've even hiked up some of the cliff dwellings."

Bailey stopped and planted her hands on her hips. "Your mom would have a fit if she knew that."

"Well, she doesn't, and if she finds out, I'll know who to blame."

"Well, I hope you won't do it again," Elizabeth said. "That is totally dangerous."

Elan shook his head. "We'll see about that."

Disaster!

"We need to leave!" Halona called to the others the next morning.

"Where's Elan?" Bailey asked as she climbed into the Suburban.

"He's not feeling well," Halona explained. "He's staying home to rest."

"Maybe that hike yesterday was harder on him than he thought," Elizabeth said as she buckled her seat belt.

When they arrived at Earth Works, Bailey took over Elan's job of sweeping the front sidewalk while Elizabeth dusted the shelves and pottery inside. Before long Bailey heard the familiar voices of Paco and the other boys who teased Elan.

"Oh, look!" Paco taunted. "Elan has a girl doing his work for him. Must have been too hard for him."

"It just so happens Elan is sick today." Bailey was immediately sorry she had given them the satisfaction of an answer.

"Aw. Isn't that too bad." Paco used his best baby voice. "Hope the delicate little thing gets better soon so we can pound him into the ground!" The baby voice morphed into a growl.

The other boys laughed. Bailey shot poisonous darts from her eyes. She was steaming mad but didn't say anything else. The boys rode off, still laughing.

As soon as Bailey finished sweeping, she went back into the store and pulled Elizabeth into the back hallway. "I'm going to give that dorko a shocko if he's not careful."

"Huh?" Elizabeth frowned.

"That mean guy, Paco, came back on his bike while I was sweeping."

Elizabeth laughed. "Paco the Dorko? That's pretty funny. Not nice, but funny."

"Well he's not too nice. I can see why he gets Elan mad."

"Just let it go," Elizabeth advised. "They're gone now anyway."

Bailey nodded. "While we're here, we should study that ancient pot again," she said. "I keep thinking after our hike yesterday that maybe some of the landscape on the pot will look familiar."

The girls went to the shelf in the hall to look again.

"I know what you mean." Elizabeth leaned so close to the pot her nose almost touched it. "But there were way more trees and dry, scrubby bushes where we hiked than

56

there are on this pot. It can't possibly be the same area."

"But the place on the pot has to be close," Bailey said. "This is where the Tses' ancestors are from. They didn't move that far away when the drought hit. They only moved closer into town."

"It just looks so different."

"I wonder if Kate found anything else out about the pot since she printed the pictures we sent." Bailey scratched her head.

"I hope so, or I'm afraid we may have run into a dead end." Elizabeth turned when she heard the bell on the front door ring. "Sounds like Halona's got customers."

Bailey looked at the pot on the shelf once more, twisting her neck to see as far around the side of it as she could. "It's no use. I can't see enough of it without picking it up."

"Bailey?" Halona called. "Could you girls please come and wrap these purchases while I ring them up?"

"Sure thing," Bailey answered.

Bailey and Elizabeth joined Halona behind the counter and pulled out a stack of white paper squares from underneath.

"Pastor John, I'd like you to meet my cousin's daughter, Bailey, from Illinois. And this is Elizabeth, Bailey's friend from Texas. Girls, this is John Whitcomb, pastor of the church down the street."

Bailey shook the pastor's hand. "Nice to meet you, sir.

This is a beautiful vase you're buying."

"You can call me Pastor John. The vase is a birthday present for my wife, Lelana." Pastor John smiled broadly, but then put his finger to his lips. "So no telling if she comes in here."

"Our lips are sealed." Bailey giggled.

Halona bagged the wrapped vase. "Here you go," she said as she handed the bag to Pastor John.

"Thanks, Halona." Then to the girls, "If you're still in town on Sunday, come on over to the church and visit us. Bible classes are at 9:30, and services start at 10:30."

Bailey's shoulders sagged. "I wish we could come, but we leave on Thursday."

"Well, next time you visit then." Pastor John smiled pleasantly. "It was nice meeting you."

Bailey's phone vibrated as she waved good-bye. She pulled it from her pocket. "Hello?" Bailey strolled to the back of the store, her phone pressed to her ear. "Hi, Kate!"

Elizabeth followed Bailey to the studio where they'd taken their first pottery lesson.

"Okay, we'll hang on." Bailey whispered to Elizabeth, "She's going to conference all the girls in, so get ready to answer your phone."

Elizabeth pulled her phone from her jeans pocket and it rang in her hand seconds later. "Yes, I'm here. Can you hear us?"

"I think we've got everyone," Kate said. "Bailey?"

"Check."

"Alex?"

"Check."

"Sydney?"

"Check."

"McKenzie?"

"I'm here."

"Elizabeth?"

"I'm here, too."

"Good," Kate said. "What's going on with you guys? Anything new?"

Bailey sighed. "'Fraid not. We went on a hike yesterday with Elan to the Puye Cliff dwellings. We thought some of the area might resemble the scenery on the ancient pot, but nothing looked familiar."

"We're starting to feel this may be one mystery we aren't going to be able to solve," Elizabeth said.

"Don't give up yet!" Kate said. "I have good news and bad news. Which do you want first?"

"The bad news," Bailey said.

"Okay. Remember I told you I was going to print out the pictures you sent me so I could study them better?"

"Yes." Bailey looked nervously at Elizabeth.

"Well, I did print them out, and they looked great. So I laid them out on the floor to examine them. Biscuit came running into the room and got her muddy paws all over them."

"Oh no!" Alex said. "Are you going to have to reprint them?"

"I'm not sure." Kate cleared her throat. "Here's where the good news comes in. Or at least it may be good news. I'm not sure."

"Let's hear it!" Sydney said.

"Well, the funny thing about the muddy paw prints on the picture is that it almost looks like trees painted onto the scenery."

"I don't see where you're going with this," McKenzie said. "How could that be good news?"

"I think I see where she's going," Sydney said. "Think about it. The Santa Fe landscape had to have changed over the last few hundred years or so since that pot was made."

"Oh, I get what you're saying." Elizabeth's eyes sparkled at Bailey. "Trees and bushes and cactus plants would have grown in since then, so it may look entirely different than the pot's picture."

"Bingo!" Kate said. "And that's exactly what the picture looks like to me with the muddy paw prints on it."

"Why don't you send us photos so we can see them with Biscuit's paw prints? Then we'll get a better idea of what the area might look like now."

"I already did." Kate giggled. "Check your e-mail."

The girls burst out laughing.

"You're really on top of this!" Bailey said.

"Anyone else have anything to report?" Elizabeth asked.

"No, I'm still researching the public records on the Tse family," Alex said. "Haven't turned anything up yet that's of interest."

"Sydney, any news on the Native American code talkers?" McKenzie asked.

"Only that the Navajo Indians were the ones who did the code talking in World War Two," Sydney said. "I don't find any connection that would tie them or their code to the Pueblo Indians."

"All right," Bailey said. "Let's keep working on this. Thanks for calling, Kate. Your tip about those photos may crack this case."

Kate laughed. "Just doing my job. Or at least Biscuit was!"

"We're working at the shop right now, but we'll check our e-mail as soon as we have time," Elizabeth said. "We'll let you know if the picture resembles anything we've seen so far."

"Okay," Kate said. "Keep us posted."

Bailey and Elizabeth said good-bye.

"Good thing I brought my laptop along," Bailey said. "I thought we might get bored, so I brought it in case we wanted to play games while my mom worked."

Bailey typed in her username and password, and Kate's

e-mail popped up with photo attachments. Elizabeth scooted her chair closer.

"There it is," Bailey said.

"Boy, that's amazing!" Elizabeth leaned in to get a better look. "Those muddy paw prints really do look like trees."

Bailey laughed. "Who knew Biscuit was such an artist!"

"This looks a lot more like the area we hiked yesterday with the 'trees' added," Elizabeth said.

Bailey squinted her eyes and pointed at the mountain to the right in the picture. "I wonder if this could be the mountain beside the Puye Cliff dwellings."

"I'm not sure." Elizabeth shook her head. "It looks more purple than that mountain. I thought it was brown or black."

"Maybe you're right." Bailey had another idea. "Or maybe it was just the lighting when Kate took the shot."

"I'm not sure the shape of the mountain is right." Elizabeth's eyebrows narrowed in thought. "Wasn't the top flatter than this?"

Bailey nodded. "I think you're right. Maybe the painting on the pot isn't where we went hiking after all." She clicked the picture off and closed the laptop.

Halona wandered into the pottery studio. "What are you girls up to?"

"We were checking our e-mail," Bailey said.

"Ready to see how the pots you made yesterday look now that they've dried?"

"Yeah!" Bailey pushed the computer to the end of the table, out of the way, while Halona got the pots from out back and brought them to the table.

"Now we get to paint them?" Bailey stood up and down on her tippy-toes.

"We glaze them," Halona said. "Have you thought about what colors you want to use?"

"I want mine to be like the sunset on your family pot, so I'll choose pink, orange, and yellow."

"I just want blue and green on mine," Elizabeth said. "Those are the colors in my room."

"Blue and green it is," Halona said as she got out big bottles of glaze and poured a little of each color into cups. She pulled paintbrushes from a drawer and laid them on the table by each girl. "What color do you want the inside of your dishes to be?"

"Pink, please," Bailey said.

"I think I'll make mine blue."

Halona poured some pink paint into Bailey's dish. "Pick up your bowl and swirl it around to make the glaze coat the bottom."

Bailey did as she was told.

"Now tip your dish on its side to get the glaze on the sides." Halona watched as Bailey let the pink glaze cover the sides of her dish.

Halona then poured blue glaze into Elizabeth's bowl,

and Elizabeth covered the inside in blue.

Bailey dipped her brush into the pink glaze and started working on her sunset. "I wish these colors were brighter." She couldn't disguise her disappointment as she looked at her painting.

"They will be after we fire them in the kiln," Halona replied.

Elizabeth cocked her head. "Guess that's a good thing to remember when we disappoint ourselves with the way we sometimes act. Just like the colors we paint on these dishes, we don't always shine like we should. But we're a work in progress. God isn't finished with us yet."

"You are wiser than your years, Beth," Halona said. "We always have room to grow and improve, don't we?"

"So the next step is firing them?" Bailey asked.

Halona nodded. "Yes. I'll turn on the kiln."

"When Mom and I bake cookies we set the oven at 375 degrees," Bailey said. "What temperature do you set the kiln to cook the pots?"

Halona laughed. "Much hotter than your kitchen oven. The first firing, the bisque, is usually at 900 to 1,000 degrees."

Bailey's eyes widened. "That's hot!"

"Yes it is," Halona agreed. "That's why you must never play around the kiln."

"How long do you bake it?" Elizabeth asked.

"Usually about eighteen hours." Halona set the oven.

Bailey's jaw dropped. "Eighteen hours! Seems like they'd be burnt to a crisp by then."

"If they were cookies they would be!" Halona teased.

"Do you use special potholders to take them out?" Beth asked.

Halona shook her head. "No. We let them cool in the kiln for two to three days before we remove them."

Bailey could hardly believe her ears. "So our pots won't be finished until we have to leave?"

"I'm afraid not," Halona said. "Making pottery is a slow process. There are many steps, and each one takes time."

"Wow. Now I understand why each piece is so special," Elizabeth said. "Especially that beautiful one handed down from generation to generation."

Halona smiled. "We take great pride in our work. For a pot to last hundreds of years as that one has only proves the excellent craftsmanship of my people."

"That's for sure!" Bailey said.

A ding at the door followed by baby cries told them they had customers.

"I'd better get back out to the front of the store," Halona said. "But I thought we should get those pots started so they'll be ready for you to take home with you on Thursday."

"Thanks for helping us," Elizabeth said. "I'm learning a lot."

"Me, too!" Bailey said. "Like never try to bake a pot and

a batch of cookies in the same oven!"

Halona laughed, her dark eyes twinkling, and hugged Bailey. "It's so good to have you here. You make me laugh in a tough year when laughter is hard to find." She gave Bailey one more squeeze and went to the front of the store.

"I was thinking," Bailey said to Beth. "Maybe we should compare the pictures Kate sent us with the actual pot. We might spot something we missed before."

"I guess it couldn't hurt," Elizabeth said. "Let's log back on."

Bailey opened the laptop and pulled up Kate's e-mail. Soon the pictures appeared on the screen.

"Let's take it to the shelf where the pot is." Elizabeth picked up the computer.

"Okay. I'll turn out the light." Bailey flipped the switch by the door.

The two slipped into the hallway where the shelf containing the pot stood. Beth held the computer beside the pot. "What do you think?" she asked.

"I think the lighting is terrible in this hallway," Bailey said. "And the light from the computer is making the colors on the actual pot look weird."

"Go turn the light back on in the studio and leave the door open to see if that helps," Elizabeth suggested.

Bailey flipped on the light, pushing the door open as far as possible. "Is that any better?"

"A little," Beth answered. "I wish the shelf was on the other wall. The light shines more on that side." Elizabeth was distracted by the noisy cries of the baby in the store and the sound of its mother trying to comfort him. "Sounds like it's someone's naptime," she told Bailey.

Bailey nodded absently. "I think we should hold the pot in the light," Bailey said. "It'll only be for a minute."

"Bailey!" Elizabeth warned. "Don't you dare even think about picking up that pot."

"Come on, Beth." Bailey faced her friend, hands on her hips. "Don't be such a worrywart."

"I am not a worrywart," Beth said. "I just know right from wrong, and we were told not to touch it."

Bailey reached out and touched the pot with one finger. "See? Nothing happened. You're blowing this thing way out of proportion."

Elizabeth's face was getting red. "Here. You hold the computer. It'll keep your hands busy."

"You're doing a fine job with it." Bailey wouldn't take the laptop from Beth but moved toward the shelf. "I'm just going to take the pot in the light for a second." She put her hand out to grab the pot.

"Bailey! No!" Elizabeth whisper-yelled while moving in Bailey's direction to stop her. Instead, she bumped the computer. Bailey's hand slipped and knocked into the pot, sending it crashing to the floor.

The girls looked at each other, eyes wide with fear.

"Now look what you made me do!" Bailey frantically picked up pieces of pottery from the floor, thankful it had broken into five neat parts rather than shattering into a million pieces.

"Me!" Fury filled Elizabeth's eyes. "This wouldn't have happened if you had just done what you were supposed to!"

"We can glue it back together and no one will ever know," Bailey said desperately.

The bell on the door rang again. More customers.

"Bailey? Elizabeth? Could you come give me a hand?" Halona called.

"S—sure, Halona," Bailey replied. "W—we'll be right there." She looked around wildly, wondering what to do with the broken pottery pieces she held. "Come on!" Bailey hurried back into the studio and stuffed the fragments into a lower cabinet against the wall.

Elizabeth set the laptop on the table and closed it. Taking a deep breath, she followed Bailey to the front of the store.

"Here, will you wrap these like you did earlier?" Halona handed a shallow bowl to Bailey and a narrow vase to Elizabeth. "Are you girls okay? You look a little pale."

Bailey giggled nervously and tried to smile. "Sure. We're fine, aren't we, Beth?"

Elizabeth lowered her head, but nodded. She took the vase from Halona and carefully started wrapping a paper square around it.

Aiyana bounded through the door, a plastic bag swinging from each hand. "I got the supplies you asked for, Mama."

"Thank you, sweetheart," Halona replied. "You can put them in the studio. The clay goes in the lower cabinet."

Bailey followed Aiyana with her eyes, and then wiped her sweaty hands on her jeans before picking up the bowl to wrap it. Her hands shook as she set the bowl in the center of her paper square. She could hear Aiyana singing in the studio. Bailey pulled one corner of the paper up and stuffed it into the center of the bowl, then another.

She stopped, hands in midair, when Aiyana screamed.

The Treacherous Summit

Aiyana's scream from the studio froze all activity in Earth Works. Halona rushed to the back and was met in the hallway by Bailey's mom, who'd raced out of the office. Together, they hurried into the pottery studio where Aiyana stood dazed, holding the broken pottery pieces in her hands. The cabinet door stood open, and the newly bought clay sat on the floor in front of it.

"Aiyana, what is it?" Halona went to her daughter.

Bailey and Elizabeth quietly appeared in the doorway and stood with Bailey's mother.

"The pot! Our key to riches. . .it's broken!" Tears poured down the little girl's face.

"Wha– There must be some mistake." Halona took the pottery shards from Aiyana's hands. She turned the pieces and looked at the painted pictures. "It can't be!"

The bell on the front door rang as it opened.

Paco's friend, Willy, burst into the store looking for Halona. "Come quick! It's Elan! He's in trouble on Puye

Cliffs! He's losing his footing, and I think he's going to fall. You've gotta come!"

Halona left the pottery pieces on the countertop and hurried out the front door, not bothering to turn the open sign to closed as she locked the door. She hoisted Willy's bike into the back of her Suburban while he and the others buckled up for the trip to the cliffs.

"He's climbing the side of the cliff like they used to do in the ancient rite of passage," Willy explained when they were on their way. "I think he's trying to prove his manhood by scaling the cliff. Sort of his own personal rite of passage. But he's slipping a lot, and I don't care if he gets mad at me. Someone needs to make him get down."

"He has nothing to prove," Halona said, defiance and fear gripping her voice. "He's more man than most boys his age."

Willy said nothing.

"Is anyone else there?" Bailey asked.

"Paco was there when I left."

Bailey closed her eyes and shook her head. That could only mean trouble.

Halona sped out of Santa Fe and into the desolate area that took them to Puye Cliffs. She swung her car into a parking space on the tourist side of the cliffs, and they ran to the place Elan had showed Bailey and Elizabeth, where the ancient rites of passage used to be held.

Willy looked up and pointed. "Whoa. He's a lot higher now than when I left." Willy walked away to where Paco stood by his bike.

"Elan!" Halona cried when she saw where her son was. "You must come down!"

"I can't!" The tremble in Elan's voice gave away his fear.

Halona snatched out her cell phone and dialed. "Chief Maska. We need your help. Elan is scaling the Puye Cliffs. You've got to talk to him. Yes. . . Thank you."

"Is he coming?" Bailey's mom asked.

"Yes. He'll be here in just a few minutes. He lives nearby."

"Aiyana, did you know he was planning to do this?" Halona asked.

"No," Aiyana replied. "He talked about proving to those boys that he was a man, but I didn't think he'd do something this crazy."

"What boys?" her mother demanded.

Aiyana shrunk back. "He didn't want me to tell," she said.

"You must tell."

"Paco and his friends have been bothering Elan almost every day since school let out. They tell him he's not a man."

Halona's mouth gaped, and tears filled her eyes. She nodded at Aiyana and hugged her. "It's okay. You did the right thing to tell me."

Bailey spoke up. "He told Beth and me about the ancient rite of passage and acted like climbing the cliffs wouldn't be hard to do. We told him we were glad the tribe dropped that tradition so he wouldn't have to do it."

"We even told him we thought he easily qualified as a man since he helps you so much and already has a job," Elizabeth added. "But I guess we didn't convince him."

"No one should have to tell him," Halona said. "He should know inside himself."

"Elan, come down!" Tears pooled in Aiyana's eyes. "We need you to help take care of us!"

"Hang on, Elan! Help is coming!" Bailey called. Even as she spoke, Elan took another step higher.

"He's not giving up," Elizabeth said. "He's determined to do this."

More boys from town had apparently heard about the daredevil rock climbing attempt and gathered at the foot of the cliff to watch. A slight breeze moved the dry, hot air.

"Boy, word sure travels fast," Bailey said to Elizabeth. "Dorko and his pals must have called all their friends."

Elizabeth didn't seem to hear. She was busy looking at the area around them. "Bales, look at this place."

"Yeah, so what? It's the same place we saw yesterday when we came with Elan."

"But think about the pictures Kate sent us," Beth said. "It looks just like this!"

Bailey viewed the landscape with fresh eyes, imagining it without all the trees and bushes. "You're right! This could be the site shown in the sunset painting on the ancient pot!"

The girls' conversation was interrupted when a white pickup truck pulled up. A man in a uniform jumped out. Gazing up at the cliff, he gave Halona a quick hug. "I see he's gone quite a ways up already."

"Yes, he has. Thank you for coming, Chief Maska." Halona wrung her hands as she watched Elan go still higher. "I don't know what to do."

"He's proving his manhood," Chief Maska said. "We can only wait and pray."

"Don't you think we should try to talk him out of it?" Bailey asked.

"Has anyone tried that yet?" the chief asked.

"Yeah, we tried, but he wouldn't listen!" Aiyana wailed.

"Then that is your answer." Chief Maska's eyes stayed on Elan. "We'll let him finish. He's climbed too high to come down safely now."

"But he could fall! Or even die!" Halona's voice rose.

The chief placed his strong hands on Halona's shoulders to calm her and looked into her eyes. "The Great Spirit will show him the way."

Elizabeth spoke up. "I don't know about the Great Spirit, but I know my God was strong enough to protect Daniel in the lion's den, and He opened up the Red Sea like a book to protect the Israelites from the Egyptians who were chasing them. I know He can hold Elan against that cliff and keep him from falling, too."

Bailey's mom put her arm around Elizabeth and squeezed her shoulder.

Bailey cupped her hands around her mouth and shouted, "You can do this, Elan! God will help you!"

"You can do everything through Him who gives you strength!" Elizabeth added. "The Bible says so in Philippians 4:13." She winked at Bailey.

"Yeah, Elan! Be strong and courageous," Bailey said. "For the Lord your God is with you wherever you go. Even up the side of a cliff!"

Elan looked down over his shoulder, then up at the rest of the cliff above him. He inched his right hand up the cliff wall until he found a handhold. He did the same with his foot. Over and over, he repeated the motion. Soon he was three-fourths of the way up.

"He looks so small up there." Sweat dripped down Bailey's face, and she wiped it with her sleeve. "I bet he's as high as my dad's four-story office building downtown!"

"If he makes it to the top, how in the world will he get back down?" Elizabeth wondered aloud.

"One step at a time, child," the chief told her.

Bailey noticed Paco and his pals had grown unusually quiet. She nudged Elizabeth and nodded in the boys' direction. "Dorko doesn't have such big things to say now, does he?"

"Nope." Elizabeth smiled. "This stunt has really shut him up. Let's keep praying Elan doesn't fall. And that Paco learns a lesson from this."

Bailey turned at the sound of rocks falling and gasps from the crowd. Her hands flew to her mouth.

"Oh no!" a woman behind her screamed.

Elan had lost his grip and slid about five feet down the side of the cliff. He caught himself on a tree rooted in a crack in the rock wall.

"I can't watch!" Halona wailed. Bailey's mother put her arms around her sobbing cousin.

"Deep breath, Elan," the chief called. "Steady yourself. You're okay."

Elan appeared to listen. Clutching the branch, he searched for a foothold. Then he laid his forehead against the cliff.

A man wearing jeans and a polo shirt hurried to Halona. "I came as soon as I heard."

"Pastor John!" Halona grasped his outstretched hand like a lifeline.

The pastor then shook hands with Chief Maska, who told him Elan was determined to prove his manhood by climbing Puye Cliffs.

"All we can do for him now is pray for his safety," the chief said.

"That I can definitely do," Pastor John replied.

Bailey shook the pastor's hand, too. "Elizabeth and I have been trying to give him extra courage and strength by telling him Bible verses that have helped us."

"Yeah," Elizabeth said. "Just the other day when Elan took us hiking out here and Bailey and I practically tripped over a rattlesnake!"

Pastor John grinned. "I think that's an excellent plan. You can't go wrong with God's Word."

"It has superhero powers in it that transfer to you when you believe," Bailey said seriously.

"That's true, if you're referring to God as the superhero," the pastor said. "I never quite thought of it that way, but I think you're on to something there." He smiled and ruffled Bailey's silky black hair. "So how about if we call on some of that supernatural strength to help Elan now?"

"Let's do it!" Bailey said and high-fived Pastor John.

She, Elizabeth, and Pastor John joined hands in a little circle. Bailey prayed first.

"Dear God, we are afraid for Elan. Protect him. Help him find the right places for his hands and feet as he climbs. Give him strength to hold on. Most of all help him not to fall and to trust in You. Amen."

Elizabeth went next. "God, thanks for being here with us. We know You're helping Elan right now, but he needs to know that You're the only Father he needs to show him how to be a real man. Give him courage to make good choices. Keep him safe. In Jesus' name. Amen."

Pastor John squeezed the girls' hands as approaching sirens wailed in the background. "God, I can't possibly say it any more eloquently than these girls have, but please be everything Elan needs in his life—his Protector, his Father, his Strength, his Confidence. May he turn to You in times of difficulty and uncertainty. May his heart belong to You. Bring him down safely to his mother. In Your Son's strong name. Amen."

Bailey looked into Pastor John's face and saw a tender smile. His eyes were moist, and he hugged them. "Thanks, girls. I know God heard our prayers and is already answering them in the way He knows is best."

"He's almost to the top!" someone yelled.

Bailey saw that in about two more reach-and-step movements, Elan would indeed be to the flat mesa at the top of the cliff. "You're almost there, Elan!" she shouted. "You can do it!"

By now a TV news helicopter hovered overhead. Police cars and fire trucks came next, sirens blaring, standing by in case emergency medical care was needed.

Elan reached one last time, and his arm landed over the top ledge. He pulled himself up and swung his leg onto the landing.

"You did it!" Elizabeth whooped.

Elan stood, his arms raised in victory.

Halona's cell phone rang.

"Mom! I made it! I proved myself a man!" Elan was talking so loud that Bailey could hear him through the phone.

"I am so proud of you, even though you scared me to death," Halona said. "Don't you ever try anything like this again, do you hear me?"

"I won't," Elan promised. "I'm worn out and all scraped up. I'm ready to be brought down."

Chief Maska stood right next to Halona. He tapped her on the shoulder and motioned for her to give him the phone, which she did.

"Elan? It's Chief Maska."

"Did you see me, Chief? I made it!" Elan jumped up and down on the mesa plateau.

"I saw you. You did a remarkable job getting up there."

"I was just telling Mom that I'm tired and all scraped up and ready to be brought down now."

"Brought down?" Chief Maska smiled wryly. "Elan, you've only done the first part of proving your manhood. Being a man means continuing even when you're tired, doing what's right even when you're hurt, and taking responsibility for your actions and choices. You must now come down from the mountain on your own, not expect someone to rescue you."

"What? I can't make it! I'm too tired. I can't do it!"

With that, Bailey saw Elan drop in a heap on top of the mountain.

One Step Closer

"You *can* do it, Elan." Chief Maska spoke gently. "I will show you another way to come down that is easier than the one you took up. Walk to your right until you see a boulder the color of the sunset."

Elan slowly stood and looked around him, cell phone still against his ear. He then followed the chief's directions. "I think I see it."

"Good. Now climb over it and follow the small path that winds to the left."

Step by step, the chief guided Elan down the mountain until finally, a half hour later, he emerged at the bottom, tired and ragged. Halona grabbed him in a hug before the paramedics checked him over.

"Elan!" Bailey rushed to him. "You made it! Are you okay?"

"I think so. Just a little beat up." He raised up his hands, scraped and raw, for her to see. "My knees are bloody, too. And I think I have blisters on my feet, but not as bad as if

I'd climbed barefoot like many of my ancestors."

Halona hugged him again. "I'm just glad you made it down in one piece."

Paramedics bandaged his wounds and listened to his heart.

"I guess there's no doubt that you're a man now," Bailey said. "We knew it before, but this should take care of any questions anyone may have had about you." Her eyes flitted in Paco's direction, and Elan smiled.

"So no more taking risks like that!" Halona scolded. "You could have been killed, and where would that have left Aiyana and me? We need you."

"I know, Mama," Elan said. "I won't do anything like that again. I know that a real man needs to be responsible, not just brave."

The paramedic helped Elan to his feet. "Okay, son. You're good to go."

"Come on. Let's get you home." Halona wrapped her arm around Elan and led him toward the car.

"Hey, Elan!"

Elan swung around to see Paco, Willy, and several other boys coming toward him. He scowled until Paco extended his hand.

"I was wrong." Paco's smile brightened his usually gloomy face. "You're tougher than I thought."

Elan shook Paco's hand, wincing as his bandaged

fingertips met Paco's grip.

Paco let go. "Sorry."

"No problem."

"Well, we'll see you around." Paco and his buddies jumped on their bikes and took off toward town.

"Who was that?" Halona asked.

"Just some guys from school." Elan kept walking toward the car.

"Were they the ones who teased you?"

Elan glared at Aiyana.

"I had to tell!" Aiyana cried.

"Yeah, they're the ones," he admitted. "But it doesn't look like they'll give me any more trouble."

"You should have told me," Halona said. "I'm sure we could have come up with a better solution than you risking your life."

As the Tse family—plus Elizabeth, Bailey, and her mom—piled into the Suburban, a sense of dread filled Bailey. With the excitement over, she suddenly remembered the broken pot.

"Halona, about the broken pot Aiyana found in the cabinet at the store," Bailey began. She figured she may as well come clean with the whole awful truth and face the consequences now.

Halona looked at her in the rearview mirror. "Oh, yes! I'd forgotten all about it in my worry over Elan."

"I broke it, and I'm terribly sorry." Bailey felt hot tears prick her eyes.

"What pot?" Elan asked.

"The pot of our ancestors!" Aiyana blurted. "The one that held the key to riches!"

"How'd *that* happen?" The accusation in Elan's voice was unmistakable.

"I—I wanted to look at it in better light. So we could figure out if the painting on the pot was of an area somewhere around here."

Elizabeth spoke up. "It wasn't all Bailey's fault. We both knew we shouldn't touch the pot, but we were equally curious. As she reached for the pot, I accidentally bumped into her and made her knock it over. That's when it fell to the floor and broke. I'm sorry, too."

"Bailey!" Mrs. Chang's face meant business. "You girls have gone way over the boundaries with your sleuthing this time!"

"I'm sorry," Bailey said softly. "I'll try to fix it. I think it will glue back together."

"Still, the damage is done. 'Sorry' and a little glue won't fix hundreds of years of history." Mrs. Chang shook her head.

"Bailey," Halona said gently. "It's okay. It's true the pot meant a lot to our family. But I think God put Elan on the side of that cliff today for more reasons than just to prove his manhood."

Bailey looked at the rearview mirror where she could only see Halona's kind eyes looking back.

"I think He put him there just at that time so I could see this situation from a different perspective." Halona paused. "The pot was very important to us, but not as important as our family or the lives we live. Elan's life was on the line today and, by comparison, that pot isn't worth the clay it was made from."

Tears spilled down Bailey's cheeks. She looked at Elizabeth and saw tears in her eyes, too.

"I don't know what to say," Bailey whispered. "Thank you."

"Yes, thank you," Elizabeth echoed. "We'll do whatever we can to repay you and repair the damage."

"I know there's really no way to do that." Bailey wiped her tears with the palm of her hand. "But you can bet we'll try our best."

"I know you will," Halona said.

●—●—●

That evening, Bailey sat cross-legged on the floor of the bedroom with her computer in her lap and chatted with the other Camp Club Girls on the CCG chat room.

> Bailey: *It's been one of the most miserable and wonderful days all rolled up into one.*
> McKenzie: *How so?*
> Bailey: *I'm almost embarrassed to tell you.*

Alex: *Go ahead, Bales. Spill it.*

Bailey: *I broke the ancient pot.*

Elizabeth: *With my help.*

Kate: *Shut up.*

Sydney: *No you did not!*

Bailey: *Yes I did, sorry to say.*

Alex: *How'd that happen?*

Bailey: *I wanted to compare Kate's paw print pics to the pot.*

Kate: *And?*

Bailey: *The lighting was bad, so I decided to take it into the light.*

Elizabeth: *But I told her not to, and when she reached for the pot, I accidently bumped her. It fell to the floor.*

Sydney: *Oh no! what happened?*

Bailey: *Halona called us to come help her, so we picked up the pieces and put them in a cabinet.*

Alex: *That doesn't sound good.*

Elizabeth: *Just as we went to help her, a kid came in saying Elan was in trouble.*

Bailey: *Elan was scaling Puye Cliffs without ropes or tools to prove his manhood.*

Sydney: *You're kidding.*

Elizabeth: *His people used to do that as a rite of passage.*

McKenzie: *Did he make it to the top?*

Bailey: *Yes, but it was scary. He slipped a couple of times.*

Elizabeth: *After he climbed down. his fingers and knees were bloody.*

Alex: *Gross! TMI!*

Elizabeth: *Sorry.*

McKenzie: *So what about the pot? Did you get in trouble?*

Bailey: *On the way back from the cliffs, I confessed.*

Elizabeth: *We apologized, though we knew it wouldn't make anything better.*

Sydney: *How'd the family take it?*

Bailey: *Mom was mad. Can't blame her.*

Elizabeth: *Halona was cool.*

Bailey: *She said Elan's climb showed what was important.*

McKenzie: *Amazing.*

Kate: *Any consequences?*

Bailey: *Not too bad. Mom took my phone away. That's why we're chatting instead of calling.*

Elizabeth: *Do you have anything to report?*

Alex: *I found the Tses owned a turquoise mine north of the northern point of New Mexico in the Jemez Mountains.*

Bailey: *I thought the mountains around here*

were the Sangre de Cristo Mountains.

Sydney: *Sangre de Cristo. I learned those words
in my Spanish class. They mean "Blood of Christ."*

Elizabeth: *Impressive, Syd!*

Alex: *Bales, from what I read, the Sangre de
Cristo Mountains are the most important
mountain range in New Mexico, but the east
side of the Jemez Mountains is where the
Puye Cliff dwellings are.*

Bailey: *So that probably explains why I've heard
more about Sangre de Cristos.*

Elizabeth: *Alex, did you find out anything about
the deed?*

Alex: *It was issued in 1848 to a man named
Hakan Kaga.*

Elizabeth wrote the name and date on a paper lying on
the nightstand.

Bailey: *Good work, Alex! I'll ask Halona if she's
ever heard that name.*

Alex: *Don't bother. I already found out that it
was Halona's maiden name.*

Bailey: *Awesome!*

Elizabeth: *Anything else?*

Alex: *That's it for me.*

McKenzie: *I don't have anything.*
Bailey: *OK. If any of you come up with anything,
     call Beth's phone or e-mail us.*
Sydney: *Will do.*
Kate: *C U l8r.*

Bailey signed off. "We could do a bit of research on the name Hakan Kaga ourselves."

Elizabeth's green eyes twinkled. "Just what I was thinking." She typed the name into her search engine. Most of what popped up was genealogical information, which she scanned. "Looks like Hakan was Halona's great-great-grandfather."

"Nothing about a turquoise mine?" Bailey asked.

"Not on this site. I'll keep looking." Elizabeth scrolled down. "Aha."

"What?"

"It says the Suquosa Mine was mined by the Kaga family from the 1600s. Somehow when people began officially purchasing land, it was bought by someone named Taime Wapi. It was bought again by Hakan Kaga in 1848. He worked the mine and passed it on to his family after his death. He was only fifty-eight when he died."

"That's not very old," Bailey said. "Does it say how he died?"

Elizabeth kept reading. "Hmm. It says he suffered injuries

in a mining accident, but doesn't say what the injuries were. But the accident happened the same year he died."

"I bet that's no coincidence."

"No." Elizabeth replied. "It might have caused his death."

"Can you find a death certificate?"

"I'm looking." Beth scanned the listings. "Here. Hakan Kaga. Cause of death: injuries sustained in mining accident."

"So he died, then the mine was passed to his family from generation to generation until now it belongs to Halona and no one can find the deed to prove it." Bailey shook her head. "Can you find out when the mine shut down?"

Elizabeth typed in "Suquosa Mine." She clicked on the first entry that came up. "It gives a brief history of the mine. Let's see here. . . . It says the mine was haunted by the deaths of many workers in the early 1900s and finally shut down due to drought and safety issues in 1925."

"Anything about where it was located?" Bailey leaned forward.

"Not really. Just that it was in the Jemez Mountains in northern New Mexico."

Bailey growled. "I wish they were more specific!"

"Something has to give pretty soon," Elizabeth said. "I feel like we're close to the solution, but somehow just can't see it yet."

"Me, too. We have to keep our eyes and ears open even

more than ever."

"I think we need to ask God's help," Elizabeth said. "We haven't been the best at seeking Him first."

Bailey was quiet, then nodded. "You're right. We've been trying to do this all on our own and forgot to put God first."

The girls bowed their heads and Elizabeth prayed aloud. "God, we're stuck on this mystery, and we need Your help. If You want us to solve this, would You please show us the pieces to the puzzle that we're missing? It would help Halona and her family so much if we could find that deed to the mine and prove her to be the rightful owner. Thank You for listening to us and helping us. In Jesus' name. Amen."

"There." Bailey said. "Now we're even one step closer to the solution."

The Secret Compartment

Wednesday morning at Earth Works, after their store-opening chores were done, Bailey and Elizabeth pulled out the pottery pieces from the cabinet.

"The pot seems even older now that it's broken." Bailey laid the pieces on the table and brushed off her hands. "I feel like we've just found these old relics on an archaeological dig!"

"Seriously, that's something to think about," Elizabeth said. "As old as this pot is, we should be extremely careful in handling it and studying it, just like the archaeologists would. We'd hate to damage it even further and lose an important clue in the process."

"You're right." Bailey went to the countertop along the wall and opened a drawer. She returned to the table with two small paintbrushes. "These should help us uncover clues without touching the pot too much."

"And what about some gloves, so oils from our skin don't get on the pot when we do have to touch it?"

Elizabeth asked. "I think the part that's painted will be protected, but I'm afraid our skin oils could discolor the plain, unpainted clay."

"Good thinking. I'll see what I can find." Bailey scrounged through drawers and cabinets until she found what looked to be Halona's gardening gloves. "These should do the trick."

"Perfect."

Bailey slipped on a pair of gloves and picked up a paintbrush.

"Wait!" Elizabeth said.

"Now what?"

"We should spread out some old newspaper on the table to make our cleanup easier."

Bailey sighed. "Cleanup? You're as bad as my mother." She started to grab a couple sections of newspapers from a pile sitting in the corner, but then reconsidered. "What if the newsprint comes off on the pot?"

"You're right. We shouldn't use that."

"We could use the same paper that we wrap the pots in when someone buys them," Bailey said. "I'll run and get some from under the counter." Bailey hustled out to the front of the store and, after getting Halona's permission, returned with a small stack of the wrapping paper. They spread the sheets out until the tabletop was covered. "Satisfied?"

Elizabeth laughed. "Yep! If we can't keep our mess on all

this, then it's a project we probably shouldn't do."

"Let's get started." Bailey gingerly picked up her favorite piece—the one with the sunset painted on it—and set it in front of her. It still had some of the pot's bottom attached to it, so it stood up as if it had never been broken. Bailey dusted off the small painting with her paintbrush, then turned the pot to dust the inside. As she turned it, she noticed a little hole only about a half inch long, exposing what seemed to be a pocket built into the pot near the top, almost like a wall within a wall.

"Check this out!" she told Elizabeth.

"What?"

"This side is hollow." Bailey stood to peer down at it.

"Of course it is," Elizabeth replied. "Pots have to be hollow to hold anything."

"Not like that," Bailey said, irritation creeping into her voice. "The actual side of the pot is hollow, like it has a pocket or a secret hiding place or something. There's a space only about a quarter of an inch wide between the two walls."

Elizabeth raised her eyebrows and stood to look at the piece Bailey was inspecting. "Wow! I see what you mean!"

"Why do you think they made it like that?" Bailey asked.

Elizabeth ventured a guess. "Maybe to hold something important, like today's safety deposit boxes do?"

Bailey had her eye right up to the hole. "I can't see if there's anything in there."

"You need a flashlight or something."

Once again, Bailey rummaged through drawers and cabinets. "It's no use. I can't find one."

"How about if I shine my cell phone light on it while you look in?" Elizabeth suggested.

"It's worth a try."

Elizabeth opened her phone and shone the light just above the hole in the side of the pot, but Bailey's head kept blocking the light. "Your head's in the way," Beth told her.

"That's where it has to be if I'm going to be able to see in," Bailey said. "Why don't you move the light?"

"'Cause I don't have anywhere else to move it to where it will shine into the hole!"

Bailey thought for a moment. "How about if we stick something in there to see if we feel anything inside?"

"Great idea!" Beth said. "We need something small, but long enough, like a pencil or pen."

"I think we should use a pen so we don't risk making marks on the inside with a pencil."

Elizabeth nodded. "That wouldn't be good."

Bailey stuck a black ballpoint pen down into the hole and moved it around.

"Feel anything?"

"I'm not sure." Bailey moved the pen again. "Maybe."

"Let me try." Bailey stepped aside and Elizabeth pushed the pen into the hole and wiggled it. "I see what you mean.

It's hard to say for sure since there's not much wiggle room, but I think something's in there. It sounds different than if the pen were just hitting against the clay pot. Muffled." She pulled the pen out, and powder from the dry surrounding clay came out with it.

"You just made the hole bigger!" Bailey said. She put a gloved finger at the edge of the hole between the two pocket walls and brushed more powdery clay out.

"Do you think we should really break this pot more than we already did just to satisfy our curiosity?" Elizabeth asked. "I mean, isn't that what got us into trouble in the first place?"

Bailey peered into the little hole, not hearing Beth. "Almost there. . ." Another brush with her finger and a couple more with the paintbrush. "I can see it!"

"See what?" Elizabeth squealed. "What is it?"

"I don't know, but there's definitely something in there."

"So now what do we do?" Beth asked.

"We brush away more of the side until we can get it out." Bailey kept working on it, and Elizabeth did her part by blowing the dust out of the way. Finally, Bailey tried to put her index finger and thumb in the hole to pull out whatever was inside, but they wouldn't fit.

"We need some tweezers," Beth said.

"Oh! I saw some in the drawer." Bailey was up in an instant. "I figured they probably used them for adding beads and stones to the pottery." She retrieved the tweezers and twisted them this way and that to try to grab onto the hidden contents. "I think I have it!"

"Be careful," Beth said. "Don't let it go."

Bailey pulled the item to the hole and they saw for the first time that it was something resembling folded dark brown leaves. "What in the world?"

Elizabeth tilted her head to try to determine what it was. "Pull it out."

"I'm not sure I can without ripping it or damaging it somehow," Bailey said. "But I have a feeling this brown part is protecting something inside it. So maybe it doesn't matter if it gets torn."

Beth brushed some more of the side away to enlarge the hole. "There. Try that."

Bailey gently pulled the tweezers and whatever was in their grasp through the hole. The brown wrapping was more pliable than they thought it would be, and only tiny pieces chipped off as it was birthed through the gap in the pot.

Electricity charged between the girls as they looked at the brown leafy package.

"I've heard that people used to use certain kinds of leaves to wrap things to protect them against moisture." Bailey's hands trembled as she gently unfolded the leaves to reveal its contents—a yellowed document with the word *Deed* written across the top in fancy curlicue writing. With great care, she lifted the deed out of its protective cocoon. Some of the words were faded, but she could clearly read the words "Suquosa Mine" and "Hakan Kaga."

Elizabeth's jaw dropped and she high-fived Bailey. "We found the deed to Halona's mine!"

Bailey couldn't contain the huge grin that stretched across her face. "Should we tell her right away?"

"Maybe we should see if we can find the mine first. What good is the deed if there's no mine anymore?"

"You're right." Bailey nodded. "We don't want to get her hopes up only to disappoint her later."

"We have to find out where that mine is," Elizabeth said. "Surely there must be an old map online somewhere."

"Or in the public records at the county recorder's office," Bailey offered.

"I'd think that if it was on public record, the Tses would have already found it. It can't be that easy." Elizabeth looked at the table with the broken pottery pieces. "We'd better clean this mess up before we start looking for the map."

"What'll we tell Halona about not putting the pot back together?" Bailey asked.

"We'll tell her the truth." Elizabeth gathered the wrapping paper covered with pottery dust. "That we found some information we needed to check out before we can finish. If she presses us, we'll just have to trust God that she won't be too disappointed if we can't find the mine."

Bailey brought the trashcan to the table. "Yeah, we sure don't want to glue the pot back together and not be able to show them where we found the deed. I think she'll be happy that we found it even if we don't find the mine right away."

"I do, too." Elizabeth carried the broken pottery pieces back to the cabinet, then rolled up the wrapping paper and dumped it into the trash. "But I think she'll be overjoyed if we find both!"

Bailey looked the room over. "We've got everything picked up, but what should we do with the deed?"

"I can put it in my bag," Elizabeth said. "No one will look in there, and it's big enough not to bend it."

She tucked the document into her bag. Then Elizabeth opened her laptop to look for a map of the mine's location. Bailey sat next to her to help her look. They clicked on several old maps and found nothing that showed Suquosa Mine. Then they clicked on one more link and found what they were looking for.

"There it is!" Bailey said, pointing at a tiny black dot.

"I can't believe it," Elizabeth said.

"Looks like it's close to where we were at the Puye Cliffs."

"I don't remember seeing anything that looked like a mine in that area, though Elan did say there used to be some up there." Elizabeth pushed back her blond hair. "I hope this isn't another dead end."

"We won't know until we try to find it," Bailey said.

"What are we waiting for?"

"A ride." Elizabeth laughed. "We can't walk there from here. It's too far."

Bailey groaned. "We don't have any time to waste. We leave for home tomorrow! Maybe my mom would take us to Halona's house, and we could walk from there," she suggested. "It's really slow here at the store today. I've only heard the bell ring once or twice all morning."

"It's worth a try. Let's go ask."

"Hi!" Aiyana skipped into the studio. "What are you doing?"

Bailey looked at Elizabeth nervously.

"We're getting ready to see if my mom will take us to your house."

"Why? Are you sick?"

"No," Bailey said. "We have something we need to do."

"What is it?" Aiyana's dark eyes grew.

Elizabeth and Bailey looked at each other, then Beth nodded to Bailey.

Bailey took her little cousin's hands in hers. "Aiyana, remember when you told us a secret about the pot and the things your ancestors said about it?"

Aiyana bobbed her head up and down.

"And you asked if we would keep your secret?"

"Yes." Aiyana's face was somber.

"Would you do the same for us?" Bailey asked her. "Keep a secret?"

99

A wide grin sliced Aiyana's face, and her eyes snapped. "Sure!"

"Okay, then," Elizabeth said. "Bailey and I need to go back to Puye Cliffs to try to find the mine that belongs to your family."

"But you can't tell!" Bailey reminded her.

Aiyana looked ready to burst with excitement. "I won't!"

Elizabeth patted her on the back. "Good girl. That's why we want Bailey's mom to give us a ride to your house—so we can hike to the cliffs from there."

"Oooh. I won't tell, I promise." Aiyana pressed her lips together and pretended to lock them and throw away the key.

"We want it to be a surprise for your mom if we can find it," Bailey added. "Understand?"

Aiyana nodded, lips pursed.

"Okay." Bailey turned to Elizabeth. "Let's go find my mom."

"I'm going to leave my bag in the studio," Elizabeth said. "I'm sure no one will bother anything in it."

She winked at Bailey, who smiled back.

Mrs. Chang was in the office working on the books. Her fingers flew over the keyboard, while she intently stared at the bookkeeping program on the computer.

"Mom, could you run Beth and me back to the house?"

Mrs. Chang looked up. "What on earth for?"

"We have something we need to do that we can't do here."

"Like. . . ?" Mrs. Chang prompted.

"Like. . .something we can't really tell you about yet." Bailey hedged with a smile. "It's sort of a surprise. But I promise it's nothing bad."

"Have you talked to Halona about this?" Mrs. Chang asked. "You're supposed to be helping her."

"Not yet," Elizabeth said. "We thought we'd find out if we even had a ride before we asked her."

"Besides," Bailey added, "the thing we need to do would help her more than us being here at the store."

Mrs. Chang eyed the girls suspiciously, a faint smile playing at the corners of her mouth. "You're up to something."

"We are!" Bailey admitted. "But it's a surprise!"

Mrs. Chang sighed and gave in to that smile. "Oh, all right. If it's okay with Halona."

Bailey hugged her mom and kissed her on the cheek. "Thanks! You're the best."

●—●—●

The second the car stopped in front of the Tses' house, Bailey and Elizabeth jumped out.

"I have my cell phone if you need us." Elizabeth held it up for Mrs. Chang to see.

"Part of what we have to do involves a hike, but don't worry," Bailey told her. "We'll take water, sunscreen, and Beth's phone."

Concern flitted across Mrs. Chang's face. "Don't make me sorry I brought you here."

Bailey laughed. "We won't. Thanks for the ride. Love you." She blew a kiss to her mother.

"Now," Elizabeth said as Mrs. Chang drove away, "let's gather our things and get going."

"We need to print out the map first," Bailey reminded her.

"Right. I'll do that while you get the water and sunscreen."

With the sun already hot at ten-thirty in the morning, the girls set out on their hike.

CHAPTER 9

Looking for the Lost Mine

Bailey and Elizabeth chatted easily as they started out.

"The sky here in this big open space is so much bluer than in Peoria," Bailey said.

"I know what you mean." Elizabeth pointed up. "Look at that cloud. It looks like the breeze is just carrying it along, not a care in the world."

"It's a gorgeous day!" Bailey loved the feeling of the warm sun on her skin. She was glad they'd remembered to put on sunscreen.

"Look! A roadrunner!" Elizabeth said. The leggy bird darted this way and that before disappearing behind a rock formation. A hummingbird with its iridescent green head zipped around in the distance.

"It's a regular wildlife preserve around here!" Bailey joked.

"Well, hopefully we won't see any wildlife we *don't* want to see, like coyotes or javelina."

"Or snakes!" Bailey added cheerfully. "Hey, we haven't told the other Camp Club Girls about finding the deed yet!"

"Oh, yeah." Elizabeth snatched her phone from her pocket. "I'll call them right now." Once she had them all conferenced, she hit speakerphone so Bailey could hear, too.

"Okay," Elizabeth began. "We have some big news to report."

"Let's hear it!" McKenzie said.

"Remember we told you we were going to try to piece the broken pot back together?" Bailey asked.

"Yeah. . . ," Sydney replied.

"We started on it, but had a minor distraction." Bailey winked at Elizabeth.

"Did we ever! Bailey found a hidden compartment in the piece that had the sunset painted on it."

"A hidden compartment?" Kate whooped. "You've got to be kidding!"

"Nope," Bailey said. "The side with the sunset was hollow, sort of like a second side hiding behind the one we could see, making a pocket that could hold things."

"Was there anything in it?" Sydney asked.

Bailey and Elizabeth grinned and kept walking.

"As a matter of fact, yes!" Elizabeth said.

"What was it?" some of the girls asked in unison.

Bailey tried to sound casual. "Just a dirty old deed to Halona's turquoise mine."

All four of the girls screamed and talked at once, and Biscuit barked excitedly.

"You're kidding!" Kate said. "I can't believe it—and neither can Biscuit!"

"What did it look like?"

"That's insane!"

"Are you sure it's the real thing?"

"I know. It's almost too good to be true!" Bailey's voice registered her enthusiasm. "But it really was the deed we've been looking for!"

"Unbelievable!" Alex said. "Was Halona thrilled?"

"We haven't exactly told her yet," Elizabeth said.

"Haven't told her? Why not?" McKenzie sounded incredulous.

"We thought it would be best to find the mine first," Bailey explained. "What good is a deed to something if it doesn't exist?"

"I see your point," Kate said. "It would only get her hopes up, and if you can't find it, she would be really disappointed."

"Exactly." Bailey climbed over a rock, then took the phone from Elizabeth so she could do the same.

"So what's the next step?" Alex asked.

"We found an old map online showing where the mine used to be," Bailey said.

"Was the map hard to find?" Sydney asked. "I looked for it a little when I did my research on the code talkers, but didn't find one that showed the old mines in the area."

"It took a bit of searching, but not too bad," Beth said. "We're just glad we found it. We go home tomorrow, you know, so time was getting short."

Bailey kept a steady pace as they talked. "We're on our way to Puye Cliffs now to see if we can find the Suquosa Mine. It's supposed to be close to there."

"I thought you sounded a little winded." Sydney's giggle rippled across the line. "You've got to get in better shape! I'll have to take you running with me next time we're together."

Elizabeth groaned. "I can't wait."

"Anyway, we'll let you know if we find it," Bailey said.

"You have to be careful around mines, you know," Kate said.

"Yeah, we know," Elizabeth said.

"No, seriously," Sydney added. "We had a special speaker come to our school and talk about that. You shouldn't go into them. They can have holes as deep as skyscrapers. Not to mention that animals or snakes may have decided to make their home in them."

Bailey watched the color drain from Elizabeth's face as Sydney continued.

"Plus, miners may have left explosives behind that could go off with the slightest touch." Sydney made a sound like a bomb exploding. "Just like that, you're gone."

Bailey imagined spit flying when Sydney imitated the explosion. "Hey! I think you got me wet with that noise!"

The other girls howled with laughter.

"No joke. I saw a movie once where a guy got trapped in a mine and there were poisonous gases and pockets with no air," Alex put in. "Of course he was near death, but then was saved just in the nick of time."

"Good to know," Elizabeth said, her color still off. She gave Bailey a nervous half-smile. "We'll keep all those things in mind."

"We probably won't need to go into the mine anyway," Bailey said. "We just want to find where it is so we can take Halona there." She hoped the girls' stories hadn't scared Elizabeth out of searching for the mine altogether.

Sydney used her best snooty voice, and Bailey could imagine her nose in the air. "All right, then. You have our permission to go."

McKenzie giggled. "But call us when you find it. I've never seen a real mine before, and I want to hear all about it."

"You mean *if* we find it," Bailey corrected.

"No, I mean *when* you find it," McKenzie said. "Think about it. If you can find an old deed that's been lost for generations hidden in a secret compartment of an ancient pot, this should be a piece of cake!"

"You do have a map, after all," Kate added. "Don't forget to use it!"

Elizabeth smiled. "I guess you're right. Thanks for the vote of confidence."

"We'll call you *when* we find it," Bailey said. "Bye!"

Elizabeth hung up and tucked her phone back into her pocket.

"Look at that!" Bailey pointed to a lizard doing push-ups on a nearby rock. "It must be time for aerobics!"

"We have lizards in Texas," Beth said. "I've heard they do that to cool off. Which reminds me, we've been walking for almost an hour. Let's take a rest."

Bailey plopped to the ground and gulped a long drink of water. "It seems like we've been walking forever."

Elizabeth pulled her hair up into a ponytail. "I know. But it can't be too much further. I remember when we came with Elan the Puye Cliff dwellings were just beyond those big boulders. I can see them in the distance, so we're probably over halfway there."

Bailey nodded, then shook her head back and forth, back and forth. Her hair swung around her head like fringe.

Elizabeth watched her curiously. "What are you doing?"

"Providing a breeze!" Bailey's swinging hair slapped first one cheek, then the other.

Elizabeth laughed. "You're too much!"

"Can you feel it?" Bailey's head continued to swing.

"Okay, sure. I can feel a slight breeze." Beth put both hands on the sides of Bailey's head to stop her. "All right. Now that you've cooled us off, we'd better get back at it."

"I guess." Bailey smoothed her hair back in place. "We

want to get to the mine and back before everyone comes home from Earth Works."

"Besides, if we find the mine, we'll be anxious to tell Halona about it and show her the deed." Elizabeth smeared on some fresh sunscreen while Bailey slathered on some cherry lip balm.

"I can't wait to see the look on her face." Bailey smiled.

The girls walked on, sweat running down their backs and foreheads. Before they knew it, they were to the cliff dwellings.

"If I remember right, Elan said the old mines were over that way." Bailey pointed to the right of the ruins.

"That's what I remember, too, so it must be right." Beth looked at the map they'd printed. "Looks like that's where it would be on this map, too. Let's go check it out."

The hard earth was cracked from baking in the sun. Tufts of dry grass and spiny bushes miraculously grew from the cracks. A stiff breeze kicked up, and a tumbleweed rolled past Bailey and Elizabeth.

"I feel like we're characters in an old western movie," Bailey teased.

"Hopefully we won't run into any gun-toting outlaws!" Elizabeth pretended to draw guns from her holster and shoot. Then she blew off the tips of her index fingers and returned them to their holsters again.

Bailey giggled. "Pretty good! And I thought *I* was the

one who should be an actress!"

Elizabeth hopped onto a good-sized rock and surveyed the area. "Let's start looking over here."

The pair split up and searched for any sign of a mine on the mountain, moving rocks as they went.

"Beth, come here!" Bailey called. "I think I may have found something."

Elizabeth hurried over.

"See? There's some rusted barbed wire around those rocks."

"It must have been put there years ago to keep people away from something," Elizabeth said. "Let's see if we can move it out of the way and get to the rocks behind it."

Bailey took one section of the barbed wire in her hand, and Beth held it about six feet down from her. Taking great care to keep the sharp barbs away from their arms and legs, they tugged and pulled, ripping up old weeds entangled in the wire from their dry roots. After several minutes of yanking at the sharp wire, the fencing was torn away from the rocks, and they stepped on it to bend it toward the ground.

"Ouch!" Bailey looked down at the drop of blood trickling down her calf. "It got me!"

"Shoot!" Elizabeth said. "And we were trying to be so careful. Does it hurt?"

"Not too bad. Do we have any tissues?"

Beth dug in their fanny pack. "No, I don't see anything." She looked around trying to find something to use in its place. "Stay here. I'll find something you can use."

Elizabeth walked a ways along the base of the cliff. Bailey saw her bend down and pick up something, then start back toward her. The stream of blood had almost reached her ankle and was beginning to dry.

"Here," Elizabeth said, handing her a handful of semi-dry leaves. "It was the best I could find."

"Thanks." Bailey took the leaves. "It'll be better than nothing." She sat down and dabbed the wet blood with the softer leaves and scrubbed the dried blood off with the rougher ones. "That worked pretty good," she said when she finished. She stood up and was ready to get to work. "Good to go."

"Now we just need to move some of these rocks." Elizabeth lifted one and tossed it aside.

"I don't want to freak you out, Beth, but remember that snakes, lizards, or bugs may be hiding under them. We should warn them so they can get out without feeling too threatened by us." Bailey threw a stick toward the pile of rocks. A startled lizard zoomed away.

"Anybody else in there?" Elizabeth threw a small rock.

They waited a moment, but there was no more movement.

"I guess if there are any rattlers, we'll know it when we hear them." Bailey stepped forward and lifted a rock.

111

Instantly, the ground beneath it swarmed with bugs. "Ewww!" Bailey chucked the rock away.

"Well, as gross as that was, I'd rather see that than a snake any day." Elizabeth moved another rock and then another. Bailey joined in, and soon they had half the rocks out of the way, and a hole in the mountainside began to emerge. Elizabeth tossed another rock aside, and two grasshoppers flew up at her. "*Aaaaaa!*" she screamed.

Bailey jumped. "What?"

Elizabeth sighed. "Oh, that scared me. Turned out it was just a couple of grasshoppers."

Rock by rock they unstopped the hole until it was almost big enough for them to crawl through.

"We've found the mine!" Bailey squealed.

"I just hope it's the right one."

"Let's make the hole big enough that we can walk into it," Bailey said.

"Hold it right there." Elizabeth stopped working, her hands on her hips. "We are not going into that mine, remember?"

"Oh, I know." Bailey wiped the sweat from her forehead with her sleeve. "But we want to be able to see into it without lying on our stomachs, don't we?"

Elizabeth paused with her lips pursed. "I guess these rocks would be pretty hot to lay on," she said. "Some of them burn my hands just tossing them out of the way."

They returned to their work, moving more rocks though their hands were scraped up. Sweat poured down their red faces.

"Look! I think we've moved enough rocks that we can step into the mouth of the mine," Bailey said. "Let's go!"

Elizabeth hesitated.

Bailey knew what she was thinking. "We won't walk into it, Beth, but it won't hurt to stand at the mouth so we can see inside."

Elizabeth frowned. "I'm not sure that's safe."

"Of course it is," Bailey said. "It's only three feet from where we were just moving rocks."

Beth looked at the rock pile and the hole in the mountain. "Okay. . .but we aren't going to go any farther than that. Got it?"

"Of course." Bailey frowned, annoyed at her friend's overprotective nature. "Believe me, I don't want to get trapped in an abandoned mine any more than you do."

The girls swigged some water. As they stood on the rock pile, Bailey noticed a partially obscured piece of weathered wood poking out toward the bottom of the mine's mouth. She pushed the rocks away to reveal a dilapidated sign that said "Suquosa."

"Beth! This is it! We've found Halona's mine!"

Elizabeth took Bailey's hands and they danced on the rocks, moving their bodies more than their feet.

"Whoohoo! We did it!" Elizabeth threw a kiss heavenward. "Thank You, God!"

Still holding hands, the girls stepped down off the rocks and into the mine's mouth.

"I can't believe we're standing in what was once known as the best turquoise mine around." Bailey looked all around her. Sunlight lit the mine's opening, but darkness so thick you could almost touch it loomed before them. Cobwebs hung at the sides of the entrance, and tiny bugs exposed to the first light they'd seen in years scurried away.

"The shade feels wonderful," Elizabeth said. "My skin will never be the same after all the sun it's had this week."

"I know what you mean." Bailey rubbed her arm. "Even though I'm not nearly as light-skinned as you, I'm glad to be out of the sun, too."

"I wonder if this is how Jonah felt when he looked at the belly of the whale." Elizabeth wrapped her arms around herself.

"It does feel like we're in the open mouth of some kind of a monster." Bailey shivered.

As they stared into the darkness before them, a rumble groaned deep and low. Bailey looked up and saw dust fall from the mine ceiling. In the shadow, she saw a mix of confusion and fear wash over Elizabeth's face. Suddenly, they felt the ground vibrate, and tiny rocks pelted their faces.

"Earthquake!" Bailey screamed.

Earthquake!

Bailey grabbed Beth's hand and dashed toward the opening they'd just unearthed. The ground shook and rolled.

Bailey tilted off balance and tumbled to the ground. Elizabeth toppled over her, pinning her arm to the hard rock. Rocks fell around them, and dust filled Bailey's lungs, making it impossible for her to breathe. She wheezed and gasped, then felt Elizabeth's hand pulling her to her feet.

"Get up! We have to get out of here!" Elizabeth rolled off Bailey.

Bailey frantically searched her pants pocket for her inhaler. She puffed the medication into her mouth. Holding her breath, she pushed to her knees, then tried to get her feet beneath her, but it was no use. The girls stumbled and fell again. An avalanche of falling rock filled the entrance, blocking their way out.

Suddenly they were in total darkness, as if someone had flipped off the light switch.

Bailey blew out the breath she'd been holding, her breath returning.

"We're trapped!" The ground finally stopped moving, but Bailey trembled just the same. "We're trapped!" she said again, taking shallow, panicked gulps of air.

Elizabeth silently wrapped her arms around Bailey.

Bailey coughed, then laid her head on Beth's shoulder. Suddenly the welcoming shade of the mine felt cold and confining. Bailey shivered and lifted her head. "What will we do?" she whispered into the dark.

"I—I don't know." Elizabeth's voice sounded flat.

"See if we have a phone signal," Bailey said.

Elizabeth pulled out her phone and the light shone. "I'll try calling your mom," she said. But she couldn't get a signal.

Tears pricked Bailey's eyes. "Now what?"

She heard Elizabeth suck in a big breath and blow it out. "We need to pray," Beth replied.

The two girls snuggled closer and squeezed each other's hands.

"God," Elizabeth started, her voice shaky.

Bailey heard her sniff and exhale loudly again.

"God, we're trapped in here." Elizabeth struggled to stay calm. "We're scared and don't know what to do."

Bailey squeezed Beth's hand tighter.

"No one knows we're in here but You." Elizabeth choked down a sob. "But You're the only One who really matters anyway. We believe You have the strength and power to

116

save us, and we ask You to do that. Help us to trust You and not be afraid. Amen."

Bailey patted Beth's hand, and then the two girls dissolved in tears, hugging each other in the dark.

"We'll make it, Bales." Elizabeth sniffed loudly. "You'll see."

Bailey nodded and wiped her eyes. "I know we will."

"At least we told Aiyana we were coming here," Elizabeth said. "If we don't make it back home in time for supper, they'll come looking for us."

"But they don't even know this mine exists," Bailey moaned. "I hope they can find it."

"Maybe they won't have to," Elizabeth said.

Bailey felt Beth stand up. "What are you doing?"

"I'm going to try to get us out of here," Elizabeth said. "If we moved rocks from the outside to get in, maybe we can move rocks inside to get out!"

"Great idea!" Bailey felt her way through the darkness to the rock wall. She tugged on a rock, but it wouldn't budge. "I can't get this rock out. It's wedged in too tight."

"Maybe if we can see the wall we can spot a place to start," Elizabeth said. "You know, kind of like playing Pick-Up Sticks or Jenga. You always try the loose ones first." Elizabeth aimed her phone light toward the wall. "See anything?"

Bailey felt the rocks wherever Beth lit them up. "This one wiggles. I'll try it." Bailey scooted the rock from side to side, and then pulled. "I got it!"

"Good!" Elizabeth reached out through the dark to hug Bailey and whacked her in the head instead.

"Ow!"

"Sorry, that was supposed to be a hug."

Bailey laughed. "That's the roughest hug I've ever had."

"I'll keep my hands to myself," Beth teased. "At least I didn't try to high-five you."

"I'm thinking it wouldn't have felt much different." Bailey smiled in the dark. "Let's work another rock out."

Again, Elizabeth pointed the light while Bailey searched for a loose rock and pulled. One by one, the two girls removed rocks from the entrance to the mine.

"You'd think we'd see some daylight soon," Bailey said.

"I know. I wonder how deep this rock wall is." Elizabeth sat down on the dirt floor. "All those rocks we moved out of the way must have rolled right back into place with the earthquake."

"And then some! Bummer." Bailey plopped down beside her friend. "All that hard work for nothing."

"Well, not for nothing, really," Elizabeth said. "We got into the mine, didn't we?"

"Boy, did we. And now we're stuck here."

"Sydney failed to mention earthquakes as one of the dangers to watch out for in the mine safety talk she gave us."

"Beth?" Bailey's voice quivered. "I'm sorry I said we should come in here. This is my fault."

118

"Don't be ridiculous," Beth replied. "I would have stopped you if I thought it was really dangerous. We would have been fine if it weren't for that earthquake. Who could have predicted that?"

"I guess," Bailey said.

"Besides, I'm older," Elizabeth added. "I'm supposed to look out for you. If anything, I'm responsible for this mess we're in."

"Remember that comment you made about Jonah when we first stepped into the mine?" Bailey asked.

"Yeah," Beth said. "I remember."

"Well, I bet this is how he felt when he was stuck inside the belly of the big fish," Bailey said. "Nothing to do but to turn to God and beg for Him to help him out of there."

"You're right." Elizabeth inhaled the damp, earthy smell of the mine. "I bet that fish smelled a lot worse than this mine, though."

"Come on." Bailey stood. "We'd better get back to work. I'll hold the light this time, and you can work on moving the rocks."

Elizabeth handed the phone to Bailey and then began prying at a loose rock.

"I'm praying silently for you while you work," Bailey informed her. "Those rocks don't stand a chance!"

Bailey's hands felt raw from handling so many rocks, and the muscles in her arms were weak from lifting them. She and Elizabeth had traded off holding the cell phone light and moving the rocks, but hadn't made much progress. They were still trapped inside the dark mine.

"I remember hearing about miners who were trapped in a mine and tapped on a pipe until rescuers found them," Elizabeth said while she and Bailey rested.

"Wish we had a pipe to tap on," Bailey said. "We'll have to think of something else."

"We could always yell," Elizabeth said.

"But what if we're running out of air in here?" Bailey asked. "We'll use it up even faster if we yell."

"Better than not doing anything," Beth said.

"Yeah, but maybe there are other options we haven't thought of yet."

They sat in dark silence.

"'When I am afraid, I will trust in You.'" Elizabeth spoke quietly, as if to herself.

"Huh?"

Elizabeth spoke louder. "'When I am afraid, I will trust in You.' Psalm 56:3."

"Where'd that come from?" Bailey asked.

"My mom used to tell me that when I was only about three years old," Elizabeth said. "I was very afraid of the dark when I was little, and when she tucked me in at night, we'd say that verse together. It was the first verse I ever learned."

"Cool. Are you afraid now?" Bailey asked.

"Yes, but that verse came back to me just when I needed it."

"Mind if I borrow that verse and make it mine, too?" Bailey asked.

Elizabeth laughed. "Help yourself!"

More dark silence.

Bailey spoke. "We have to get out of here so we can tell Halona her mine is real. Are there any sticks or something we could use to poke between the rocks?"

Elizabeth walked around, shining her phone close to the mine floor. A thick wire bar about three feet long was laying about five feet away. "Yes!" She jumped up and grabbed it.

"Now all we have to do is find a place to stick it through," Bailey said.

"I don't know if there is a place," Elizabeth said. "I don't recall seeing any light peeking through those rocks, do you?"

"No, but God just provided us with a wire, so maybe He'll show us a place to put it." Bailey took Elizabeth's hand and they walked to the blocked off entrance. "Put your phone away so there's no extra light in here," Bailey said. "We'll see the light shining through better in complete darkness."

Elizabeth tucked her phone in her pocket. Hand in hand, the girls walked along the rocked-in mouth of the mine.

"I don't see any light anywhere, do you?" Bailey asked.

"Unfortunately, no." Beth sighed.

"I know! Let's back up and look from further away," Bailey suggested. "Maybe we're just too close to it to see it shining through."

The girls linked arms and stepped about ten paces back, then started walking the distance of the wall again. Bailey tried so hard to see something that she started seeing weird colors in front of her eyes.

"There!" Elizabeth said. "I think I see something."

"Where?"

"I'm pointing to it." Elizabeth put Bailey's hand on her arm and had her follow it to her pointing finger. "Put your head by mine and look down my arm."

Bailey did as she was told, her eyes following where she felt Elizabeth's finger pointing. There it was—a tiny pinpoint of light between two rocks.

"I see it!" Bailey squeezed Elizabeth's arm. "Now let's walk toward it, not taking our eyes off it until we're there."

Gingerly, they made their way to the speck of light, wire in hand.

"It's up higher than I thought," Elizabeth said, as they approached. "I hope we'll be able to reach it."

As they got closer, the light disappeared.

"It's up too high!" Bailey said. "We can't even see it when we're this close."

"Okay," Elizabeth said. "We just need to back up and find it again. Then one of us will stay back here and the other will have to go toward it."

"But we can't even see each other!"

"I'll turn on my phone and light up the mine long enough to see which way you need to go, and I'll direct you toward it," Elizabeth said. "We'll see if you can climb up the rock wall and stick the wire through it."

"It's worth a try," Bailey said.

The two backed up to where they could spot the tiny dot of light. "There it is." Elizabeth flipped open her phone and turned it in Bailey's direction. "Now you walk until you get to the rocks."

Bailey followed her friend's instructions, darkness surrounding her as she moved farther from Elizabeth's phone light. Hands outstretched, she soon felt the cool rocks. "I'm there."

"Start climbing. I'll tell you which way to go."

Bailey put the wire in her mouth so she'd have both hands free for climbing. Elizabeth closed her phone for a second to see the pinpoint of light better. Then she opened it again to spot Bailey on the wall. "Move a little to your right. You're almost right underneath it," she instructed. "You'll need to climb up about three feet."

Bailey thought of Elan scaling Puye Cliff. *This should be nothing compared to that.* Placing her foot on a rock she couldn't see, she felt for a place to grab with her right hand. She moved her other foot up to another rock and then reached for a handhold with her left hand. Little by little she moved higher.

Elizabeth shone the phone light. "You're there! It's just above your head. Stick the wire in!"

Holding on to a rock with her left hand, Bailey took the wire from her mouth with her right hand and felt for the hole. She poked over and over, only to feel the wire hit hard rock. "I can't find it, Beth! And I can't hold on much longer."

Suddenly, another low rumble began, and Bailey heard a strange creaking. She climbed down a few feet, then jumped from the wall and ran to where she hoped Elizabeth was. The ground began to shake and roll. Dirt and rocks fell around them, and Bailey heard rocks from the mine entrance shift. Frantically pawing the air to find her friend, she yelled, "Beth!"

"I'm here!" Their hands swept the air until they found one another. Huddling together, they covered their heads with their arms. Seconds later, the trembling stopped and the mine was silent. Bailey and Elizabeth slowly unfolded themselves from their fetal position.

"I think that was an aftershock," Elizabeth said. "It didn't feel as strong as the first one and didn't last as long."

"I heard a creepy creaking when I was up on the wall, so I jumped down," Bailey said. "I was afraid the whole mine was going to collapse on us!"

Elizabeth looked toward the rock wall where Bailey had been seconds before.

"Oh my goodness! Bailey, look at the entrance!"

Daylight!

Bailey looked, shocked at what she saw. Narrow slivers of light streamed through the rock wall in three places. "God is making a way out for us!" Bailey still quivered from the quake.

"Or at least making it easier to get a signal out to people who can help us," Beth said. "Do you still have the wire?"

"Yeah. I hung on to it when I jumped down."

"Good. Let's see if we can find something to tie on to it. We can use it as a flag to stick through a crack between the rocks."

"Okay," Bailey said, "but don't you think we should try to move more rocks? We might be able to get out now."

"I think we should do both," Elizabeth said. "Let's make a flag to hang out one of the openings first. Then if someone comes looking for us while we're working on the wall, they'll see where we are."

"Good thinking," Bailey said. "That way *it* can be working while *we* work!"

"Exactly." Elizabeth paused. "The brighter the flag, the better."

"I don't know if we have anything bright to use." Bailey tried to see through the blackness. "It's too dark to find anything."

Beth aimed her phone light all about the mine but didn't see anything in the dim light that they could use. "I'm going to shine the light closer to the ground while I walk around to see if I can find something."

Bailey followed behind, and the two walked slowly, painstakingly, looking for any scrap of brightly colored fabric that could be used as a flag, without going further into the mine. "Whoa! Look at this!" Bailey held up a blue rock about the size of a walnut. "Turquoise!"

Elizabeth brushed some dirt off it and held her phone close to look it over. "It's beautiful! Must be plenty of turquoise left in this mine if it's just lying around like that."

"Yeah. Here's another piece!" Bailey felt like cheering. She put the rock in her pants pocket and continued searching. "I don't think we're going to find anything we can use for the flag," Bailey said finally.

"I don't think we are either." Elizabeth started to put her phone away.

"Wait!" Bailey said.

"What? Did you see something?"

"Your shirt! It's red!"

Elizabeth pointed the light on herself and laughed. "I forgot what I wore today!" Beth suddenly grew quiet.

"You won't have to take it off," Bailey said, realizing what was troubling her friend. "Let's just rip off the pocket."

"You've got a deal!" Relief flooded Elizabeth's voice. She put her fingers into her pocket and pulled. The pocket tore halfway off. Another tug and it was in her hand. "I got it!"

"Good job!" Bailey said. "Should we just poke the wire through it or tie it on?"

"I think we should tie it so it doesn't fall off as easily. Hand it to me, and I'll do the tying."

Bailey stuck out her hand, but Elizabeth didn't take it. "Here."

"Where?" The girls searched for each other's hands, and then Elizabeth found the wire. She held it between her knees as she tied the red pocket to the end. "I'll try to tie it from the corner so more of the pocket will hang out."

"Good idea," Bailey said.

"There. I think I got it. Do you want me to climb up to put it in one of the openings, or do you want to?"

"Doesn't matter," Bailey answered. "I guess you can since you already have it."

"Here. You hold the light."

Bailey held up the phone, which dimly lit Beth's path. "I'll direct you like you did for me. Let's just pray the battery doesn't die on us."

"Okay. Let me know if I'm getting off course." Beth started climbing the wall. "At least that one hole isn't quite as high as the others. I'll try for it."

"You're doing good," Bailey encouraged. "A little to your left."

"The trick is going to be squeezing the flag through that slit." Beth climbed a little higher. "I see it. I think I can reach it from here." She took the wire, flag end first, and tried to poke it into the tiny space where the light shone through.

"That's it!" Bailey said.

"It's not going in." Elizabeth pushed it again and felt the wire go through the hole. "It's going!"

"It is, but the flag isn't," Bailey told her. "It's scooting down the wire instead of going through the hole with it."

Elizabeth groaned. "I need to come down. I can't hold on anymore." She started her descent, then jumped when she was close enough to the ground.

"I've got an idea," Bailey said when Elizabeth was down from the wall. She shivered in the cool, damp air. "We could tie the pocket to the wire, then bend the end of the wire back over the flag so it can't slip off."

"Let's try it," Elizabeth said.

Bailey held the phone light while Beth tried to secure the flag with the wire. After she bent the wire over the flag, she twisted it over the remaining wire below the red pocket. "There. That should do it."

"Want me to try taking it up this time to give your arms a rest?"

"Sure." Elizabeth took the phone back.

Once more, Bailey started up the rock wall that blocked the mine exit. "If this doesn't work, I'd say we should start moving rocks and making noise so people will hear us."

"Me, too." Elizabeth kept her eyes on Bailey in the dim light. "But I sure hope it works this time."

Hand, foot, hand, foot. Bailey made her way up the wall, wire and flag between her teeth.

"Almost there. Only about one more step and then reach."

A dot of light shone in Bailey's eyes, and she blinked against the unaccustomed brightness. She took the three-foot wire from her mouth. "I found it!"

"Good. I'll be praying down here while you try to stick the flag through."

Bailey pushed the wire flag first into the bright light. It resisted, bending the wire. She continued to twist and push until it suddenly flew through, almost making her lose her balance on her foot- and handholds. "I did it! It's through!"

"Awesome! Way to go!" Elizabeth clapped her hands as Bailey made her way back down. "Now, we start tearing down the wall."

"I need to rest a minute," Bailey said. "My arms and legs are shaky from all that climbing."

"That's okay," Elizabeth said. "You rest. I'll get started."

"I'll make noise while you move rocks in case anyone's within earshot."

"Perfect!"

Elizabeth worked on the wall, one rock at a time. Each one took a considerable amount of time as she wiggled and pulled, moving it only fractions of an inch at a time.

Bailey took her noisemaking job seriously. "Help! We're in this mine! Help! Come find us!" Finally, she stopped yelling and listened. Nothing.

"Beth?" Bailey's voice was quiet.

Elizabeth continued working on the wall. "Hmm?"

"What if they don't find us? And what if we can't get the wall moved?"

Elizabeth stopped her work and climbed her way back to Bailey in the dark. "Give me your hand."

Bailey did, and Elizabeth found it after swiping the air with her own. She sat down by her friend. "Listen, Bailey," she said. "We're *going* to get out of here."

"That's what we hope will happen, but what if we're wrong? What if they can't find us?"

"You know they'll look until they do. Nothing will stop them."

Bailey was silent. "What if" thoughts swirled around in her head like a giant whirlpool. "You're a good friend, Beth. The best."

Elizabeth squeezed Bailey around the shoulders. "So are you, Bales."

The girls sat that way for a few minutes, saying nothing.

" 'Surely I am with you always, to the very end of the age.' " Elizabeth quoted the words of Jesus. "Matthew 28:20. We're not in this mine alone."

Bailey wiped at the tears that threatened to fall down her cheeks. "I know. But I'm still scared."

"I think everything's finally catching up to us," Elizabeth said. "The hike, moving rocks, the stress of the earthquake. Maybe we should rest awhile, before starting to work on the wall again."

"My mom always says a girl can cope with things better when she's well rested," Bailey said. "Maybe things won't look so hopeless if we take a short nap."

Elizabeth laughed. "I usually hate taking naps, but that does sound pretty good right about now."

Bailey agreed, and they leaned against each other, Bailey's head on Elizabeth's shoulder. Within minutes, the two fell asleep, backs against the cold wall.

What seemed like only seconds later, Bailey and Elizabeth awoke to the sound of men's voices.

Elizabeth jumped up. "Help! We're trapped in here! Help!"

Bailey scaled the rock wall, making it to their wire flagpole in record time. She wiggled it frantically. "Over here! See the red flag moving? We're behind these rocks!"

The voices grew more distant and then faded away.

"They didn't hear us!" Bailey wailed. "I wiggled the flag! I thought for sure they'd see it."

"I know. So did I," Elizabeth said. "Did you recognize the voices?"

"No, they sounded pretty muffled behind these rocks. Did you?"

"No," Beth said. "At first I thought maybe one was Elan, but it was too deep."

"We've got to move more rocks so they can hear us easier." Bailey started working on one rock and Elizabeth on another.

"We won't give up, Bales," Elizabeth said. "We can do this."

"With God's help, we'll get out of here ourselves if they don't find us first."

"I think that catnap we took helped." Hope filled Elizabeth's voice. "I feel like I have more energy, don't you?"

"A little," Bailey's voice trembled. "I just want out. I'm sick of being in the dark."

"I know what you mean." Elizabeth worked her rock side to side. "I'm starting to crave sunlight."

Bailey pulled on her rock, her fingers burning and raw. "It's weird how cool it is in here when it's so hot out there."

"Yeah, I'm afraid we'll freeze if we don't get out before dark."

"We'll get out." Bailey stood straight. "I have faith!"

Elizabeth laughed. "I'm glad. So do I."

Bailey's rock suddenly came free, and she landed on her backside. She laughed. "I'm glad you couldn't see that, Beth."

"See what?"

Bailey explained what had just happened.

"I missed it," Elizabeth teased. "I could've used a good laugh, too!"

With each rock that was pulled out, a bit more light came in, but other rocks fell in, filling the hole they'd just made.

"We can't seem to clear enough space to crawl out!" Bailey wailed.

"Just keep at it," Elizabeth said. "We can't give up!"

●—●—●

"Hello?"

"Anybody there?"

Bailey and Elizabeth stood stock still for a nanosecond. They leaped onto the rock wall.

"Help! We're in here!" Elizabeth shouted.

Bailey reached the wire flagpole first and wiggled it wildly. "Help! Help!"

"We hear you!" the rescuer said. "Hold tight. We'll get you out of there."

Elan yelled into the rocked entrance. "Bailey! Elizabeth! It's Elan! You're going to be okay."

"Elan!" Tears sprung to Bailey's eyes. "I'm so glad to hear your voice."

"Are you hurt?" one of the men asked.

"No," Elizabeth replied. "Just tired and scared."

"Bailey? Is that you? It's Mom!"

"It's me," Bailey answered, her voice shaking. "Don't worry. We're okay now that we know we'll get out of here soon."

The girls caught glimpses of hands until a circular hole at the top of the wall spanned about two feet wide.

"Do you think you can crawl out?" a rescuer yelled into the hole.

"Sure!" Bailey said. "We just have to climb the wall, and I've already been up it plenty of times today!"

She started climbing the wall once more, wincing at the pain from her sore toes and raw fingertips. Elizabeth crawled up behind her, and when Bailey got to the top, the rescuer pulled her out as Elizabeth pushed from behind. The warm sun never felt so good on Bailey's face.

In minutes, both girls were out and hugging Bailey's mom and the Tses.

"Oh Mom, I love you! I've never been so happy to see you in my whole life," Bailey said, as she hugged her mother.

"That goes double for me!" Mrs. Chang hugged Bailey, then held her at arm's length to look her over. "You weren't hurt in the earthquake?"

"No, but that's how we got trapped," Bailey said. "The rocks fell and covered the entrance so we couldn't get back out."

"God was looking out for you, that's for sure," Halona said.

"We knew it all along," Elizabeth said. "He was right there in that mine with us, wasn't He, Bales?"

"Yep, and His Word kept coming to our minds," Bailey added.

"That's why it's so important to hide God's Word in your heart, like you've done," Bailey's mom told them. "Then it's there to draw from when you need it."

"It was pretty cool, the way that worked," Beth admitted.

"Come on," Halona said. "Let's get these girls home. They've had quite a day."

"That's for sure." Bailey turned to her rescuers. "Thank you for finding us and getting us out." She hugged them with all her might.

The four o'clock sun blazed as they started walking toward the tourists' parking lot, when Bailey remembered. "Halona!" she said. "I almost forgot. We have some good news for you!"

The Surprise

Halona swung around toward Bailey. "What good news?"

"Well," Bailey said, "when I tried to fix the pot I broke, I found a secret hiding place inside."

"What?" Halona unlocked the car doors and the group piled inside. "I can't wait to hear *that* story on the way home!"

Once they were in the Suburban, Bailey continued. "I picked up the piece with my favorite part of the painting on it, the sunset." Excitement fizzed in Bailey like carbonation in a soda. "I was going to glue it to another piece, but I noticed that the side where it had broken looked weird."

"How was it weird?" Halona asked.

"It was hollow!" Bailey raised her eyebrows. "It had a hidden wall inside the outer one, making a pocket-like compartment just behind the sunset." Bailey buckled her seat belt, and they were off.

"Was something in it?" Bailey's mom asked.

Bailey nodded. "Yes, but I'm not going to tell you what until we get back to the shop."

Halona looked at Bailey in the rearview mirror. "Well, aren't you the mysterious one?"

"I don't mean to be mysterious," Bailey said. "I just think it will be neater to show it to you instead of just tell you about it. Don't you think so, Beth?"

"Definitely," Elizabeth said. "Believe me, this is worth waiting fifteen minutes to find out."

Soon, the Suburban pulled up in front of Earth Works, and they all climbed out. Halona unlocked the store and stepped inside, where Bailey saw her wince at the sight of the earthquake damage. Her hands flew to her mouth, tears pooling in her dark eyes. The smell of pottery dust hung in the air.

"I'll never be able to afford to replace all this merchandise," she whispered.

"What about your insurance?" Mrs. Chang asked. "Will it cover it?"

"It may cover some of it, but probably not everything." Halona slumped onto a stool behind the counter. "I don't know if we can recover financially from this. We may have to shut down the store."

"Wait." Bailey strode to the studio with Elizabeth close behind and rummaged through the pieces of broken pottery in front of the open cabinet that had held the family heirloom. As she brushed shards aside, she spotted the one with the sunset painted on it and picked it up. Like jigsaw puzzle pieces from different puzzles all mixed together, the ancient pot was beyond repair.

"Where's the deed?" Bailey asked.

"In my bag," Elizabeth replied. "Remember? We put it in there so no one would find it and so it wouldn't get crumpled." Elizabeth retrieved her bag and pulled out the deed.

She handed it to Bailey. "Let's go present this to its rightful owner."

The girls walked down the hall to the store, where everyone was busy picking up broken pottery pieces, baskets, jewelry, and blankets. Elan was putting his broom to good use.

"Seems like something's missing." Bailey looked around the store and spotted the incense holder. "That's it!" She went over and lit a fresh stick of incense. "Now it smells like it should in here. It smells like Earth Works."

"We found what we wanted to show you, Halona," Elizabeth said.

All work stopped, and everyone gathered by the counter.

Bailey cleared her throat. "It is with great pleasure that I present to Halona Tse this deed to the Suquosa Turquoise Mine. It belonged to her ancestors and now belongs to her and her family."

Halona's mouth fell open. Her eyes went from Bailey to Elizabeth, then to Bailey's mom and her own children. "The deed? Is this for real?"

"It's real, all right," Bailey said. "It's what we found inside your pot." Bailey showed her the broken piece of pottery and the pocket where the deed was found.

Aiyana tugged on her mother's hand. "Mama! It's just like what your mother told you, remember? 'Behind the sunset our treasure awaits!'"

"So that's what it meant," Halona said, still stunned. "And my grandma always said the pot held the key to riches. They knew. They knew! But the specifics of it didn't get passed to the next generation." Halona hugged Bailey and Elizabeth. "You girls have solved an age-old mystery."

Her finger traced the fancy old-fashioned writing that spelled the word "Deed" at the top.

"Now we just have to find out if the mine still exists, and if so, where." Halona's eyes clouded with doubt. "It will be a huge undertaking."

"It sure was." Bailey grinned, her eyes crinkling.

"Was?" Elan asked. "What's that mean?"

"It was a huge undertaking," Elizabeth said. "But it's already done."

Confusion danced across Halona's face. "I don't understand."

"That's what we were doing on our hike." Bailey laughed. "We were looking for your mine when the earthquake hit and we were trapped inside."

"But at least we found it!" Elizabeth said.

"How can you be sure it's the right mine, the Suquosa?" Halona asked. "There are many old mines in that area."

"We're sure." Bailey's voice brimmed with confidence. "For starters, we found an old map on the Internet that showed its location, so we printed it out and took it along."

"And it led us to the right spot!" Elizabeth said. "But a huge rock pile covered the entrance."

"So we decided to move all those rocks and try to get inside." Bailey saw her mother's frown. "We know mines are no place to play around, but we weren't going to walk back into it or anything. We just wanted to see if it really was behind those rocks."

Elizabeth nodded. "Our hands got scraped up, so we were glad when we uncovered the mine's entrance. We opened it up enough to stand in it."

"And when we did," Bailey put in, "we saw an old wooden sign sticking out from behind some rocks. We moved them, too, so we could read the sign."

"What'd it say?" Aiyana asked.

"It said 'Suquosa Mine'. " Bailey folded her arms across her chest and raised her chin proudly.

"It is too much to take in," Halona said. "All of this is so unbelievable."

"This is what we've dreamed of, Mama." Elan took his mother's hands. "We can have our mine back."

"We don't even know if there is still turquoise in the

141

mine," Halona said. "That will be important to learn before we get too excited."

Bailey stuck her hand in her jeans pocket and pulled out two blue stones. "Will this be enough proof to answer your question?" She opened her hand to show the stones to Halona.

Halona inhaled sharply and tears sprung to her eyes. "It is too good to be true!" She grabbed Bailey and Elizabeth and hugged them fiercely. "Thank you! You have no idea how much this means to our family."

•—•—•

Thursday morning, while the Tses went to the county recorder's office to update paperwork on the mine, Bailey and Elizabeth called the other Camp Club Girls.

Elizabeth had her phone on speaker so she and Bailey could both hear as she conferenced in the rest of the girls.

"Mystery solved!" Bailey announced.

"No way!"

"What?"

"How'd that happen so fast?"

"Amazing!"

"Yep," Beth told them. "We followed the old map showing where the mine should be. We couldn't see it at first, but then noticed a big pile of rocks with some old rusted barbed wire around it."

"We started moving the rocks and found the mine entrance," Bailey added.

Bailey and Elizabeth recounted their work getting the mine entrance cleared.

"Wait a minute," Alex said. "You didn't go into the cave, did you?"

"We only stepped in at the edge," Elizabeth said. "We didn't walk back into it."

"But Sydney forgot to mention one thing in the safety talk she gave us," Bailey said.

"I did?" Sydney said. "What?"

"Earthquakes." Bailey waited for a response.

"Huh-uh," Sydney finally said. "You did not have an earthquake while you were in that mine!"

"We sure did," Bailey said. "And we were trapped inside for hours."

"You should have listened to me in the first place and not gone in there!" Sydney scolded.

"I know," Elizabeth said. "You were right. We had no business going in there."

"What'd you do?" Kate asked.

Bailey told them what it was like being stuck in an old abandoned mine, and Elizabeth added information about how they worked to get out and made a flag to help rescuers find them.

"Were you scared?" Alex asked.

"Totally!" Bailey said. "I was more scared than Beth. She kept telling me cool Bible verses to keep me calm. I need to memorize more verses so I'm better prepared for bad situations in the future."

"Bailey was very brave," Elizabeth said. "It was pitch dark in the mine except for when I shined my cell phone light. She did great."

"So did Beth," Bailey said, "especially for a kid who used to be afraid of the dark. We couldn't get a signal for Beth to call for help on her cell phone, but at least the light on it worked."

"We were afraid the battery would die, but we decided to trust that God would get us out safely." Elizabeth winked at Bailey. "We even prayed together in the dark."

"So how did you get out?" McKenzie asked. "Did you move all the rocks?"

Bailey told them about hearing the men's voices and how they were rescued. "We climbed out the hole they cleared, and boy, did that sunlight seem bright when we came out!" Bailey covered her eyes and laughed.

"Was Halona surprised about the deed and the mine?" Kate asked.

"We told her we had a surprise for her, but we didn't tell her what it was until we got back to Earth Works." Bailey scrunched up her shoulders.

Elizabeth continued the story. "Her store had a lot of damage in the earthquake with broken pottery all over the place. As soon as we got back there, she forgot about the surprise. She started talking about how much it was going to cost to replace all the ruined merchandise and how they might have to close the store."

"It was really sad," Bailey said. "But then I thought about the deed and the mine. I went into the studio and found the piece of pottery with the pocket to show Halona."

"And I got the deed from my bag," Elizabeth added.

"Then we presented it to Halona." Bailey couldn't stop grinning.

"She must have had kittens right there on the spot," Kate said.

Elizabeth laughed. "Practically! She could hardly believe it was real."

Bailey went on. "And then she decided she shouldn't get her hopes up too high until they found out if the mine was still around and if it had turquoise in it."

"We informed her that we found the mine and Bailey showed her the turquoise stones she had picked up while trapped inside." Elizabeth shook her head. "She was dumbfounded!"

"I've never been hugged so hard in all my life!" Bailey teased.

"What will they do now that they have the deed?" McKenzie asked.

"They're at the county recorder's office right now updating their claim." Elizabeth smiled proudly at Bailey.

"They have the deed, and she has her identification to prove it's hers."

"It didn't look like it would take much work to make it operational again, and it should pay off for them in the long run." Bailey shrugged.

"You guys were amazing!" Sydney said. "I can't believe you found the deed and the mine in only a few days."

"We wouldn't have found the deed if the pot hadn't broken," Bailey admitted. "I'd say God had something to do with that."

"And of course you guys helped, too!" Elizabeth said. "Biscuit's paw prints showed us that the landscape around Puye Cliffs really did match the pot's painting with trees added."

"Good old Biscuit, the Wonder Dog," Kate said.

"And Sydney eliminated the idea that the things Halona's grandma and mother said about the pot was some sort of code when she researched the Native American code talkers from World War Two," Bailey added.

Elizabeth jumped in. "And Alex researched all the public records on the Tse and Kaga families."

"The rest of us prayed for you like crazy!" McKenzie said.

"We know you did!" Bailey said. "We might still be sitting in that dark mine if you hadn't been praying!"

"Anyway, we just wanted to let you know that the mystery is solved, and Halona has her mine back," Bailey said.

"I'm glad you called," Sydney said. "But mostly, I'm glad you weren't hurt in the earthquake or from being trapped in the mine."

"God really was looking out for you," Alex said.

"No doubt about it," Elizabeth said.

"We go home this afternoon, so we'd better hang up so we can pack." Bailey looked at her clothes strewn all over the bedroom.

"Okay," McKenzie said. "Thanks for calling us with the good news. Hopefully, we'll have another mystery to solve soon."

"I hope so!" Bailey said. "Bye!"

—●—

Halona hugged Bailey's mom good-bye. "It was so good to see you again."

"I'm glad we could come to help out for a little while," Mrs. Chang said. "I hope you can get things repaired and replaced in Earth Works soon."

"I will," Halona replied. "I spoke with the insurance company this morning, and they're going to pay for more of it than I thought."

Halona's arms went around Bailey, then Elizabeth. "When I invited you all to come give us a hand, I had no idea how helpful you'd be."

"Thanks." Bailey held the finished dish she had made in the studio. "It was fun to learn to make pottery and work in

147

your store. I've never done those things before." She looked at her dish, which had somehow survived the earthquake, and admired the sunset she'd painted on it. "This will remind me of our time together."

Elizabeth hugged Halona. "Thanks for letting me come with the Changs."

"You girls gave me far more than a little help in the store," Halona said. "You gave me a better life for my family. I can't thank you enough."

"We're happy everything turned out so well," Elizabeth said.

"But I still feel a little guilty about breaking your ancient family pot," Bailey said.

"That's okay." Halona smiled at Bailey. "You showed us that sometimes we have to sacrifice something good to get something better. The real treasure wasn't the beautiful pot. It was what was inside, a bright future with my family."

●—●—●

A week later, back home, Bailey called Elizabeth.

"Hey, Beth, guess what?"

"I give up."

"Remember how I said I needed to learn more Bible verses so I'd have them ready in a tough situation?"

"Yeah. . ."

"Well, I've already started." Bailey smiled proudly. "Wanna hear it?"

"Sure!"

Bailey cleared her throat. " 'Store up for yourselves treasures in heaven, where moth and rust do not destroy, and where thieves do not break in and steal. For where your treasure is, there your heart will be also.' Matthew 6:20 and 21."

Elizabeth cheered. "Way to go, Bales! I'm proud of you!"

"I'm learning the real treasure is knowing God and letting Him be the boss of our lives," Bailey said. "Like when we had to trust Him in that mine."

"Wow, Bailey," Elizabeth said. "That's pretty good!"

"But I didn't really call to brag about learning a new verse," Bailey said.

Elizabeth laughed. "You didn't? Then why did you call?"

"We got a package in the mail today!" Bailey squealed.

"Cool! Who's it from?"

"Halona!"

"Did you open it yet?" Elizabeth asked.

"Not yet. I thought I should wait until I called you so we could sort of open it together, since it's addressed to us both."

"Well, open it!" Elizabeth begged.

Bailey cut through the mailing tape with a pair of scissors and tore off the brown wrapping.

"There are two smaller boxes inside the bigger box," Bailey reported. "One has your name on it, and one has mine."

"Open yours first," Elizabeth said.

"Are you sure?" Bailey asked.

"Yes! Open it!"

Bailey lifted out the box bearing her name and removed the lid. She gasped.

"What is it?" Elizabeth asked.

"It's a beautiful turquoise necklace!" Bailey said. "Wait. There's a note under it." Bailey picked up the note and read:

> *Thank you for your help at Earth Works last week. Let this necklace serve as a reminder of how much we appreciate and love you. It is made from turquoise taken from the Suquosa Mine, which is now operational again. Thank you!*
>
> *Love, Halona, Elan, and Aiyana*

"Wow!" Bailey fingered the turquoise stone. "Shall I open yours, or do you want me to mail it to you as a surprise?"

Elizabeth giggled. "Open it!"

Bailey lifted the lid and found a similar necklace and note for Elizabeth. "You're going to love it, Beth."

"Thanks for letting me come with you on that trip," Elizabeth said. "It was a real adventure."

Bailey laughed. "You can say that again. I'm just glad we know where our True Treasure lies!"

Can't wait for the next Camp Club Girls adventure. . .
here's a sneak peek into book 16.

Kate and the
WYOMING FOSSIL
FIASCO

Water, Water Everywhere!

"Kate, watch out!"

Kate Oliver jerked her arm back as she heard her teacher's voice.

Kaboosh! A large glass of water tumbled over, landing directly on the fossil plate she had just unpacked from a large wooden box.

"Oh no!" Kate squeezed her eyes shut. Surely she did *not* just spill water on a priceless artifact, thousands of years old!

"Quick. Let me dry it." Mrs. Smith, Kate's teacher, grabbed a paper towel and ran toward Kate.

Kate backed away, shaking so hard her knees knocked. "I–I'm so sorry! I didn't mean to spill it."

Of all things! She had come to the museum to help her teacher. And now she'd destroyed something of great value! Why, oh why, did things like this always seem to happen to her?

"It's not your fault, Kate," Mrs. Smith said. "I left my glass of water sitting there. I only have myself to blame."

"Still. . ." Kate's glasses slipped down her nose, and she pushed them back into place. Tears filled her eyes as she watched her teacher. How would the museum ever replace something so valuable? And would Mrs. Smith lose her new job as museum curator? A shiver ran down the twelve-year-old's spine.

"Please, Lord, don't let that happen!" she whispered.

"Wait a minute. . ." Mrs. Smith shook her head as she dabbed the fossil plate with the paper towel. "Something is very wrong here."

Kate leaned forward to look. "W—what is it?"

"A glass of water couldn't possibly harm *real* fossils," Mrs. Smith explained. "But look at this." She pulled the towel away, and Kate gasped. The fossil imprint appeared to be dissolving, slowly melting away before her eyes.

"I don't understand." Kate took her finger and twisted a strand of her blond hair, something she often did when she was nervous.

"Neither do I," Mrs. Smith said as she pulled off her latex gloves. "But I'm going to get to the bottom of this." When her hands were free of the gloves, she pulled out a magnifying glass and examined the fossil plate. After a moment, she whispered, "Oh my. This doesn't look good."

Kate grew more curious by the moment.

"Kate, see what you think." Mrs. Smith handed her the magnifying glass. Kate peered through it, taking a close look.

"Very interesting," she said. "They look like grains of

sand, only maybe a little bigger."

Kate reached into her backpack and pulled out a miniature digital camera, just one of her many electronic gadgets. She zoomed in and began taking photos, documenting the changes in the fossil as they occurred. She had a feeling these photos would come in handy later.

"Up close it doesn't even look real. Funny that I never noticed it before." Mrs. Smith touched a spot where the water had landed, then stuck her finger in her mouth. Her eyes grew wide as she looked at Kate. "You've got to be kidding me!"

"What?" Kate asked. "What is it?"

Her teacher gasped. "Brown sugar!"

"No way!" Kate took one final picture of Mrs. Smith with her finger in her mouth. "The fossil plates are. . .fake?"

"Looks that way." Her teacher put down the magnifying glass and shook her head. "I don't believe it. I simply don't believe it. These plates are on loan to the museum from a quarry in Wyoming. We're expecting hundreds of guests to visit the museum to see them. And now we find out they're not even real? This is terrible news!" She reached for a piece of paper and began to fan herself. "Is it getting hot in here?"

Kate shook her head. "Not really." She put her camera away and then looked at her teacher, trying to figure out how she could help.

"I must be nervous." Mrs. Smith paced the room. "What am I going to do?"

She paused and looked at Kate. "This exhibition was supposed to be the biggest thing to happen to our museum in years. People were coming from all over the country to see these fossils. Oh, why does something like this have to happen my first week as curator? Why?"

"I don't know, but I would sure like to get to the bottom of this," Kate said. "So, if you don't mind. . ." She pressed her hand inside the backpack, fishing around for something. Finally she came up with the tiny fingerprint kit.

Mrs. Smith looked at her, stunned. "You just *happen* to have a fingerprint kit in your backpack?"

"Yes." Kate giggled. "I always carry it with me. I never know when there's going to be a mystery to solve or a criminal to catch."

"You solve mysteries?" Mrs. Smith looked confused. "And you catch criminals?"

Kate nodded and smiled, "Along with a bunch of others called the Camp Club Girls."

She would have plenty of time to explain later. Right now she had work to do. She pulled out several other gadgets, starting with a tiny digital recorder. "I'd like to record our conversation, Mrs. Smith. You might say something important to the case."

"Case?"

"Sure. I have a feeling this is going to be a very exciting one, but I need to keep track of the information, and recording it is the best way."

"I suppose that would be fine." Mrs. Smith shrugged.

Kate turned on the recorder and set it on a nearby table, asking her teacher questions about the fossil plates. Then she pulled something that looked like an ink pen from her backpack.

Mrs. Smith looked at her curiously. "Do you need to write something?"

"No, this isn't really a pen." Kate wiggled her eyebrows and smiled. "It's a text reader. Look." She took the pen-like device and ran it along the edge of the wooden box the fossil plates had been packed in. It recorded the words STONE'S THROW QUARRY, WYOMING'S FOSSIL FANTASY LAND.

"Very clever," Mrs. Smith said with a nod.

After recording a few more words from the side of the box, Kate turned her attention back to her backpack. She pulled out the computerized wristwatch her father had given her. One of his students had invented it, and soon it would be sold in stores. She could hardly believe it was possible to check her e-mail or browse the Web on a wristwatch, but it had already come in handy several times.

Her teacher looked at Kate's gadgets, her brow wrinkling in confusion. "Why do you have all of these things, Kate? Do you really solve mysteries, or is this some sort of game?"

Kate shook her head. "It's no game. And it looks like we have a doozy of a mystery here. But to solve it, I need to contact the other Camp Club Girls."

"Camp Club Girls?" Mrs. Smith fanned herself with a piece of paper. "I'm not sure I understand. Who are the Camp Club Girls?"

"We're a group of girls who all met at Discovery Lake Camp awhile back," Kate explained. "We solve mysteries together. If anyone can get to the bottom of this, the Camp Club Girls can."

Mrs. Smith's eyes grew wide. "Really? Do you think you could help figure out who did this? That's a lot to ask of a group of girls your age."

"You would be surprised what the Camp Club Girls can do with the Lord's help!" Kate went to work lifting fingerprints from the edges of the fossil plate. Before long, she had a couple of great ones. "Perfect. Now, if it's okay with you, I need to send an e-mail to the girls in the club to see if they can help."

"Well, sure," Mrs. Smith said. "I guess that would be okay. Do you need to use one of the museum's computers to get online? I'm sure I could arrange that."

"No thanks." Kate pulled off her latex gloves and opened her wristwatch. "I can send e-mails on my watch."

"You—you can?" Mrs. Smith did not look convinced.

Kate typed out a quick note to the girls:

Emergency! Need help cracking a fake fossil case!
Meet me in our chat room at 7:00 p.m. eastern time.

She closed the watch and smiled at her teacher. "Don't worry, Mrs. Smith," she said, trying to sound brave. "The Camp Club Girls are on the case! We'll figure out this fossil fiasco in no time!"

With the tip of her finger, she reached to touch the ruined fossil plate, then stuck her finger in her mouth tasting the sweetness of the brown sugar. These plates might not be the real deal, but they sure were tasty. And Kate was convinced they contained clues to help unravel the mystery.

Suddenly, she could hardly wait to get started!

Join the Camp Club Girls online!

www.campclubgirls.com

✿ Get to know your favorite
Camp Club Girl in the
Featured Character section.

✳ Print your own bookmarks to use
in your favorite Camp Club Book!

✳ Get the scoop on upcoming adventures!

(Make sure to ask your mom and dad first!)